NELL of Branford Hall

NELL of Branford Hall

William Wise

Dial Books / New York

Published by Dial Books
A division of Penguin Putnam Inc.
345 Hudson Street
New York, New York 10014

Copyright © 1999 by William Wise
Printed in the U.S.A. on acid-free paper
First Edition
1 3 5 7 9 10 8 6 4 2

Library of Congress Cataloging in Publication Data
Wise, William, date.
Nell of Branford Hall/by William Wise—1st ed.
p.   cm.
Summary: Nell Bullen recounts the horror of
the Great London Plague in 1665 and the "Circle of Death" that
was drawn around her village to keep the disease from
spreading to neighboring towns.
ISBN 0-8037-2393-8
1. Plague—England—London—Juvenile fiction.
[1. Plague—England—London—Fiction.] I. Title.
PZ7.W778Ne 1999   [Fic]—dc21   99-19023   CIP

*To Robert—the oldest of friends,
the best of brothers*

Table of Contents

A NOTE FOR THE READER

ACKNOWLEDGMENTS

NELL of Branford Hall

Eagles' Roost

I must tell the story of The Great London Plague while I still have the chance, for I am grown a very old woman now, and am surely among the last ones left who witnessed that appalling tragedy. And perhaps the only one left who saw—as I did with my own young eyes—how the Circle of Death was later drawn around our own village of Branford, and the extraordinary things the brave villagers did in those desperate times.

I was born thirteen years earlier, about a mile from Branford village, in the year of our Lord 1652. My childhood, until I was nine, was an extremely happy one. Indeed, on those rare occasions when I thought about my place in the world, I knew myself to be one of the most fortunate children in the whole of England.

Many people would have said that I was fortunate because my family was wealthy, and we lived in a handsome, spacious manor house. I had fine clothes to wear, enough food to eat each day, and permission to play music on my mother's harpsichord, which I loved to do, for an hour every morning. And all about us were beautiful places to see and visit. There were the wooded hills that surrounded us on three sides, our orchard of fruit trees, and below the house, down in the valley, the swift, sparkling stream that raced along toward Branford village and beyond.

But my good fortune did not really lie in all these pleasant things—though they *were* pleasant things to have, to see, and to enjoy. My good fortune rested in the kind of loving parents I had—the very best mother and father, I do believe, that ever there were.

My mother was not a particularly strong or robust woman, yet she was destined to bear my father four children within less than six years. Mary, my older sister, was the first. Next there came Samuel, but he was just a name to me, for I never knew him. Like so many infants, he failed to survive his first winter, dying in early January, when only six weeks old.

After the passage of another year or so, there came Henry, who was two years my senior. He was everyone's favorite, and my own dear friend and playmate, though we were, in certain ways, very different from one another. Henry was far more lighthearted, and far less studious, than I. He loved nothing better than to walk in the woods and meadows. There, from time to time, he would introduce me to all the wild creatures, and the growing things, that he had discovered on his many rambles.

During the early summer of my ninth year, Henry was stricken with a sweating fever, and my uncle John Townley came down from London to try to restore him to health. Uncle John was one of my mother's several brothers. He was a most eminent physician, and knew a good deal of what there was to know, at that time, of medicine and medical science. But all of his knowledge proved in vain, and every cure that was attempted proved useless. On a lovely morning in July, at the very height of summer, my dear brother Henry joined Samuel in our family graveyard, behind the private chapel, at the end of the meadow.

My mother's quiet but unwavering religious faith gave her consolation. For the doctrines of the Established Church assured her that her beloved child was now with God, and in a far happier place than he had ever known during his earthly life. My sister, Mary, who held similar beliefs, often joined my mother at prayers and drew much comfort from the hours they spent together.

My father, though, had no such faith and turned to his own skeptical philosophy for consolation. One day he found me in the apple orchard, my back turned, my forehead pressed against a tree, weeping bitterly. He gave me his handkerchief—which was much larger than mine, of course—and after I had dried my eyes, he took me by the hand. Silently we climbed together through the woods until we reached the top, where there was a clearing. The place was known in Branford as Eagles' Roost, and from it you could see for miles—not so far as London, indeed, but on a very clear day for thirty miles at least.

We sat there, and I said, "Henry used to come up here, on such a day as this," and my father said, "Yes, I know, Nell."

Then I lost my self-composure again and wept, and my father waited patiently until my tears were done. Finally he said, "You miss your brother so very much, don't you?" and I said, "Yes, I do. Each and every day, most terribly."

When I had grown calmer, I said, "Father, there is something I truly do not understand. I know that Mother misses Henry and finds consolation in her prayers. And I know that you miss him just as much, yet you do not pray."

"I lack your mother's faith," he said. "So prayers would not be of any help to me."

"Then what is of help?" I asked him.

"Well, I have a consoling thought," he said, "which seldom leaves me. It is the thought that your brother Henry was a very happy child, but that quite possibly most of his brightest days were already over, and that before many more years had passed, his happiness might very well have turned to grief and sorrow."

My father paused for a time. At last he said, "Henry, you see, was so very much like Edgar, my own older brother. Edgar was the same kind of carefree lad. He loved to roam through the woods and meadows, he loved adventure, he cared little for study or learning. And Edgar came early to misery, violence, and ruin."

My father paused again. "Yes, there was Edgar, the Young Cavalier, and there was our father, the Old Cavalier, and there was me—and there was ruin enough for all three of us, I can assure you."

He looked at me and said, "Have I never told you of my family's fortunes—and misfortunes? Have I never told you how I believed I should lead one sort of life—and how I was compelled to lead a very different sort?"

I shook my head. "No, Father. You have told me nothing of such things."

"Then perhaps it's time for me to tell you now. What do you think?" My father smiled, and his eyebrow lifted slightly, as it sometimes did when he was teasing me. "Can you spare me a little of your time, Nelly?"

Whenever he called me Nelly instead of Nell, it was always a tease, so I nodded and said, "Yes, Father, I think today I can spare you the time for your recital!" Then I gave him back his handkerchief and sat there listening. And before the day was done, I had learned that I, Eleanor Bullen, a fortunate yet commonplace English girl, was actually a distant relation of two of the most famous queens in the entire history of England!

2 A Tragic Queen

I can still remember the warm summer afternoon my father and I spent, perched high above the world at Eagles' Roost. White clouds streamed overhead, sunlight burst upon us and then vanished, breezes stirred the wild grasses around our feet. And I remember my father, alternately solemn and self-mocking, caught up in a web of his own memories and his knowledge of events that had taken place years before.

The Bullen family, I learned, had originally been French. Exactly when the first of its numerous members had reached our shores, though, my father did not know. In France, and for a time in England, the name Bullen had been written "Boleyn"—and that, of course, was the way that Henry VIII's tragic second wife had spelled it, when she had been crowned Queen of England.

"Anne Boleyn!" I cried after he'd told me. "Oh, Father,

are you saying that we are her distant relatives—and therefore relatives of *her* daughter, Queen Elizabeth? Does that mean if the present king, and his brother and sister, and their various children, were all to die off, then *you* would be next in line to the throne? You would become king, and Mother would be queen!"

"No, no, no," my father laughed. "Do not fly so high, Nelly. Our connection is not nearly that illustrious or exalted!"

My father laughed again and then, little by little, began to untangle the matter for me. He'd learned about the Bullen family, he explained, from his own father, George Bullen, the Old Cavalier. Like many country gentlemen, George Bullen—my grandfather—had been enormously proud of his family name and his high position in the county. Naturally, then, he'd wished to learn everything possible about his forebears and his ancestral pedigree. So one day he'd hired a poor scholar at Oxford to search through the ancient parish records and discover just how grand his remote family connections had really been.

My father's eyes danced with merriment as he continued the tale. "That scholar was a diligent man," he said. "In fact, rather too diligent, I fear. Because when he'd finished and presented his findings, the poor Old Cavalier was distressed to learn that *our* particular Bullen ancestor had been a rather undistinguished member of the family. Worse still, the early Boleyns hadn't been aristocrats at all, but silk merchants in London, importing damasks and similar rich stuffs from the East. Mere tradesmen then—but highly successful ones, so before long they could

9

afford to wear silver buckles on their shoes, live in handsome new houses, and even marry into the nobility.

One of the Boleyns, my father told me, his expression turning grave, had managed to do even better. Sir Thomas Boleyn had been a clever, ambitious man. He'd flattered, schemed, and plotted at the Royal Court, until finally he'd seen his daughter Anne become Queen of England. And then he'd watched the tyrannical and fickle king grow weary of her, had heard that the king meant to be rid of her, and at last had learned of her bloody execution in the Tower of London.

"However," my father said, his smile returning, "*our* Boleyn ancestor was less ambitious. He never once appeared at the Royal Court, but remained in London and became a very rich merchant. Apparently his wealth so improved his manly charms that one day he took to wife the daughter of a most illustrious, though rather impoverished, country squire.

"And so," my father concluded, "in another generation or two our branch of the family turned its back entirely on trade. We became proud landed gentry, leased our acres to the local farmers, and swore eternal fidelity to the church and the king. And that, Nelly, is about the sum of it. There really is no more."

The Old Cavalier

My father, though, had told me nothing of his own high hopes and disappointments, and I soon reminded him of this. "What sort of life, exactly, did you mean to lead?" I asked him. "And what brought ruin to all three of you— to my grandfather, to my uncle Edgar, and to you?"

"It was the Great Rebellion," my father said, "that tore our country apart. Before it began, I was a fortunate young man with what appeared to be a most promising future. My father, though he cared nothing for science or literature, knew that I cared for little else. Having a generous disposition, he granted me—his second son—an annual allowance. After two years' study at Oxford I went to London, took rooms near the Strand, and continued my medical and scientific studies. My older brother, Edgar, was my father's principal heir. Being much like my father in interests and temperament, he was delighted to remain at home. There he could play his proper role as a rising young squire in the county, dealing with his tenants, raising his own crops, and improving the land he would someday inherit.

"The months that I spent in London," my father told me, "were among the happiest of my life. I was utterly absorbed in my studies, and the prospect of one day becoming a skilled physician filled me with delight. In addition I made new friends, among them your uncle John Townley, who already was a young physician with a growing reputation for his medical knowledge and skills.

"And Nelly," my father said, his eyebrow giving him away again, "I'm sure you've already guessed another cause of my happiness—the real, best cause. My friend John Townley had a younger sister named Anne. When I met her for the first time, one afternoon in Gray's Inn Walks, I did what any sensible, intelligent young man would have done—I fell instantly and hopelessly in love with her."

"And did Mother accept you at once?" I asked. "Or did she make you wait and suffer?"

"No, Nelly, she was not so cruel as some young females I could name. By a miraculous dispensation that I've never been able to understand, she found me almost as charming as I found her. Soon afterwards we were properly married, with the enthusiastic approval of both the Townley and the Bullen families.

"Then," my father said, "the Rebellion broke out, there was civil war between King Charles I and the armies of Parliament—and my own life changed forever, in what seemed the twinkling of an eye."

This time when my father fell silent, it was for a very long spell. Finally he said, "I was still in London, occupied with my studies, when the Battle of Marston Moor was fought, and the king and his Cavalier supporters—my father and brother among them—were defeated by the forces of Parliament under General Oliver Cromwell. My father had raised a company of horsemen and led them into battle. I believe he probably was the oldest rider on the field, and certainly he was among the bravest, and the most loyal to that unworthy king. He was known to Cromwell and the Parliamentary forces as a deadly enemy, and when he was cut down and killed, they rejoiced.

"My brother, Edgar, was equally loyal to the king, and attempted to carry secret messages to Scotland on his behalf. He was captured, tried as a traitor, and executed. Our family home was plundered, the house blown up with gunpowder and leveled to the ground, the land itself confiscated by Parliamentary decree. In London I found myself surrounded by the triumphant enemies of my family. I was in danger of being arrested at any time on suspicion of high treason, and I had scarcely a shilling in my purse with which to support my helpless young wife.

"At this moment the Townleys came to my rescue. They provided me with money and false papers. Disguising myself as a foreign merchant, I boarded ship one dark night, slipped down the Thames, and sailed for the Netherlands—and two years of lonely exile.

"The rest of it is quickly told," my father said. "After those two years the Townleys judged that it would be safe for me to return to England. To an obscure place somewhere in the country, but not, of course, to London and my studies, for there the enemies of my family were stronger than ever.

"Branford Hall now belonged to your mother, who had inherited it from a distant relative. Here we came to raise our family, and here I abandoned all hope of becoming a physician. Instead, I resigned myself to the destiny I always had hoped to avoid. I became a country squire and lived far from the booksellers and the theaters, the classrooms and the laboratories, and the private apartments of learned societies and learned men. Far from the literary and scientific life of the greatest city in the entire civilized world!"

"Have you not led a happy life then?" I asked him.

He smiled ruefully and said, "Of course I've led a happy life, Nell, and today I am still a happy man. I have the loveliest and most loyal of wives, and two charming daughters who are a joy to me—at least *one* of them is, when she's on her good behavior! I have a host of London friends like your uncle John who visit me, and I have a beautiful place to live. And here I have been able to pursue my own private studies. Safe from all danger, I have been able to watch the turbulent world go by—to inform myself of the trial and execution of the old king, and the reign and death, three years ago, of Oliver Cromwell. Since then it has been safe for me to return to London whenever I wished. There I have seen a new Stuart king ascend the throne. Recently, I have had my possessions restored to me, and today I am no longer beggared by my family's enemies. No, Nell, I have enjoyed a good life, and if one or two of my dearest dreams have not been realized—why, isn't that the common fate of most men?"

~ ~ ~

The afternoon was nearly over, and my father and I arose, left Eagles' Roost, and descended to our house. As we entered, he beckoned me into his study. There he opened a cabinet and took out one of the tiny enamel pictures, called *miniatures*, that he kept there.

He placed the portrait in my hand and asked me if I knew who the man was. I studied the gentleman, who had a fine mustache and beard—"Well, he's handsome enough"—and then I saw his eyes, and I exclaimed, "Oh, he has the very same eyes as my brother Henry!"

"Of course he does," my father said. "I told you they were much alike. It is a portrait of my brother, Edgar. I am giving it to you now, as a keepsake, because my brother and yours so greatly resembled each other. Thus I believe that you will cherish it, in Henry's memory, for all the rest of your days."

I thanked my father, and that night, before I put out my candle, I looked again at the portrait. Then I placed it under my pillow and held it there as I fell asleep. And it made me feel less lonely that night, and for many nights thereafter, as my father had known it would.

Fleas in the Bedclothes

With Henry gone, Mary and I began to spend more time together than we ever had before. If the weather was fair, we took long walks or rode two of my father's new Dutch horses along the narrow country lane that led to Branford village and beyond. If the weather was cold and wet, we stayed indoors and busied ourselves with household tasks, some of which I found highly entertaining.

During the summertime flies were very numerous in even the best-managed English homes, and Branford Hall was no exception. There were several excellent ways to deal with them. One was to fill a bowl with milk and the juice of two or three raw onions. The mixture attracted the flies, so that they swarmed about, tumbled in, and drowned.

If you were skillful enough, you could make fly whisks

and swat them to death, although you had to be careful not to stain the upholstered furniture or the curtains. Or you could hang up pieces of string that you'd dipped in honey, and the flies would come, get stuck, and perish by the dozens.

My favorite task, though, was one called picking-the-fleas-out-of-the-bedclothes. Mother always kept several white "flea blankets" in storage. When you spread them over a bed, the little black pests soon jumped on them, and you could catch and squash them between your fingers then and there.

But the best way to deal with fleas was to remove all the sheets and blankets from the beds, fold them up as tightly as possible, and then pack them away in a dark, locked chest. The fleas, deprived of food and air, and with no way to escape, perished quickly. Several days later you could pluck them from their former lodgings and dispose of them at a safe distance from the house, and after that— at least for a while—there would be no more fleas in your bed to plague you at night.

My mother was amused by my bloodthirsty taste in household chores, but she was not at all amused, or pleased, with my reading and the education I was receiving. One day she took me into my father's study, where she sat down and confronted him. She was not angry in the least, but was as cool and determined as ever I had seen her.

"Richard," she said, "we must talk about our daughter Eleanor."

"Talk about Nell?" my father said with surprise, looking up from the book he was reading. "Why, what in the world is there to talk about?"

"There are several things," my mother said firmly. "One is that her studies have been sadly neglected lately. In the beginning you said you would give her instruction, and to do you justice, so you did."

"Of course I did," my father said.

"You taught her to read and write, and how to do her sums."

"And she does her sums very well," my father said. "As for reading and writing, I'd venture to say there's no other girl in the county—or quite likely in the entire kingdom—who can do any better."

"But she could do so much *more*, Richard!"

My father, I believe, was as impressed with my mother's tone of voice as with her words. He thought for a time, and then said, "What else would you have her do, Anne?"

"She must have more schooling," my mother said. "Down in the village, Dr. Thomas Wentworth, our new minister, is going to accept a number of pupils, both boys and girls. Last month when you met him, you said he was an able and learned young man, and he can begin to instruct Eleanor in Latin, Greek, and French."

My father, still more surprised, looked at me and said, "Would you like to study French and the classical languages?"

"Yes, Father," I replied. "I very much would."

"And one day," my mother said, "she also would like to read some of the books in your library. When she under-

stands more, of course, and if you would be kind enough
to give her your permission."

My father's astonishment was now complete. "Is that
also true?" he said to me.

I nodded again and said, "Yes, Father. I have so few
books of my own to read now. I have the lovely Aesop's
Fables that you gave me last winter, but I've already read it
eleven times, and I have nothing else but the Bible, which
I do not care for quite so much."

My mother smiled for the first time, and then she made
the longest speech that I ever heard her make. "My dear,"
she said to my father, "you are so busy these days, manag-
ing the property, and working at your scientific projects,
like the wonderfully improved fruits that you've begun to
grow in the orchard, and the gardens of medicinal herbs
that you've learned to cultivate. You aren't always fully
aware of what is happening around you. Our Mary is fast
becoming a young woman now and, before long, will
wish to have her own home and family. She takes after
me, and someday soon, the Lord willing, she will be a
housewife and mother, and her happiness will lie chiefly
in that.

"But our younger girl," my mother continued, "has a
hunger to learn things. She takes after you, Richard, and
the mere fact that she is a girl rather than a boy does not
mean that her mind should be neglected. I know—for she
has told me—that she loves to listen to what you and her
uncle John say about medical matters, and only wishes
that now and again she might ask you one or two questions about your discussions. And I know that one day she

hopes you will think her grown-up enough to let her see what sort of things you are studying under your microscope."

My mother drew me closer to her and began to smooth my hair. "We have an unusual daughter," she said softly, "and I believe we are obliged to do our best for her."

"Of course we are," my father exclaimed, and being the spontaneous sort of man he was, he seized me by the hand and led me into his laboratory, which stood next to his study and library. There he put a pillow on his chair for me and told me to look into his microscope. And I saw the caterpillar he was studying—at least a *bit* of the caterpillar, and chiefly some of its body cells. Afterwards I thanked him, and later still, when we were alone, I hugged my mother, and thanked her too for what she had done on my behalf.

Mary was pleased for my sake that I would soon begin to attend school. But she was equally pleased for herself when she learned that she would have the congenial duty of escorting me each day to and from the Reverend Thomas Wentworth's house in Branford village. So I teased her over him, for I knew that she already fancied our young minister very greatly. After my words she blushed and said, "Oh well, yes, Nell—but he *is* very handsome, don't you think?"

I didn't have the heart to tell her what I actually thought—that Thomas Wentworth's nose was too beaky for my own taste, and the calves of his legs rather too straight, and his hair a shade of brown that I did not especially care for, and that, indeed, taking it all in all, if he were the last man on Earth, I could not be sure whether I would have him or no.

But I did hold my tongue and swallow my words, and I said, "Yes, Mary, I do think he is most admirable—and I am sure he has a fine, strong character, which is needed in a husband, and the best thing in all the world for a man to possess."

Those hypocritical words of mine satisfied my sister, and I realized with a pang that the beaky-nosed scholar who was to teach me French, Latin, and Greek had utterly and absolutely stolen my sister's heart away.

Kate

A few weeks after my mother's long speech to my father, things began to change for me. One morning my sister and I dressed with special care—she to gain the approval of the Reverend Thomas Wentworth, and I to avoid the scorn and mockery of the other students. Then off we started to Branford village and the beginning of my first term at school.

We were five scholars in all, three boys and two girls, and we studied spelling and grammar, Latin, Greek, and French at two heavy square tables, set out for us in an unused storage room at the back of the parish house.

I didn't like any of the boys. Red-haired and pudgy, Will Dunstan was twelve years old and scarcely knew how to sign his own name. He had no wish to learn anything more, his sole interest in school being to see how hard he could pinch us girls whenever our teacher wasn't looking. His father was Captain Dunstan, a hard-drinking old villain who lived on the far side of Branford village. My own father and mother did not respect the captain, so it was no difficult task for me to thoroughly detest young "Pinching Will."

Peter Ford, the apothecary's son, I detested even more. He was a toadeater, a flatterer, always trying to curry favor with Thomas Wentworth—"Oh Sir, may I carry that heavy book for you—and please let me move that heavy chair, Sir—I do so love to move heavy chairs!" It was disgustful how he behaved. One day, when our teacher was off somewhere else and Peter Ford had been particularly servile and obnoxious, I said to him, "You are a loathsome hypocritical knave!" and kicked him in the shins. I knew that I should not have done so, but it gave me much satisfaction at the time. Perhaps I repented of it later, as any good and worthy child ought to have—though I certainly would not take my oath on it now.

Lastly, there was frail little Arthur Povy, the son of Samuel Povy, the wonderfully skilled tailor who lived in Branford village. Little Arthur was a bright child, younger than I, and he already knew considerable Latin and a smattering of French.

I tried to like Arthur and sometimes felt guilty when I failed to do so. But he was a sickly creature, forever complaining about the heat of the day, which made him dizzy, or the damp of the classroom, which set his hands and feet to aching. Of course, I should have been kind to him, but I was scarcely ten years old myself, and had no great sympathy for anyone else's troubles unless they were very much like my own.

These, then, were the three boys at the Reverend Thomas Wentworth's school—"Pinching Will" Dunstan, toadeating Peter Ford, and poor sickly Arthur Povy. And then there was the other girl besides myself—Catherine Carter, Thomas Wentworth's niece. She was full of high spirits and loved to chatter as much as I did, and being the same age almost exactly, the two of us soon became the closest of friends.

Not only did Kate and I spend much time together at our village school, we also began to visit each other's homes and families. She and her uncle Thomas were welcome at Branford Hall, my mother approving of my friend, and the Reverend and my father, with many interests in common, soon becoming fast friends themselves. Occasionally after school I was allowed to stay on at the parish house. When I did, my sister usually joined me there and helped Kate's widowed mother, Mrs. Carter, supervise the preparations for supper.

~ ~ ~

Little by little, when I was free of school and my studies, I began to explore Branford village and its surroundings, and eventually I came to know many of the people who lived in the neighborhood. More than once this led to a great surprise—like my discovery that William Ford, the village apothecary, was a good and upright man and nothing at all like his knavish and servile son, the hypocritical Peter. Indeed, one day Kate and I learned the local gossip about the Ford family. To begin with, Mr. Ford did not even *look* like his son. The villagers said that some years before, when Peter's mother had visited a sick relative in a distant town, she had been "indiscreet" with one of the gallants there, and Peter wasn't really Mr. Ford's child at all!

How Kate and I goggled over that morsel of scandal. Later, when we were alone and could give vent to our feelings, we shook with laughter at the very notion of portly old Mrs. Ford ever having done such a scandalous thing—and of our servile Peter being the consequence of her sinful misdeed!

What Kate and I found, though, in Mr. Povy's tailor shop and in his home was not gossip and scandal, but something quite different.

One day after school, with Kate in tow, I entered Mr. Povy's workshop for the first time, sent there by my mother to pick up a sample of cloth that the tailor had promised to obtain for her from a merchant in London. His shop was filled from floor to ceiling with the tools of his trade; so crowded was it, indeed, that once he had wedged in the small table at which he worked, there was no space left at all that was unoccupied.

Piled high everywhere were various fabrics—rare and expensive silks and laces, yards of damask of every sort, calico and cotton stuffs, woolens and more woolens. In short, anything and everything that a man or woman could desire for suits and cloaks, dresses and petticoats, or for the furnishings of a home, was found here. And at the center of all this lovely and colorful profusion sat Mr.

Povy himself. His long, quick hands were ever in motion, stitching, clipping, measuring, cutting—a fantastic magician with needle, shears, and thread.

Then a door at the back of the workshop edged open, and our fellow pupil, little Arthur, peered in. Perhaps there was a draft of some kind, but even with his back turned, the tailor seemed to know that his son was standing behind him. He stopped work and moments later ushered the three of us into the kitchen, where Kate and I were introduced to Mrs. Povy and to Arthur's older brother, Jasper.

Kate and I spent an hour that day in the Povys' friendly kitchen, eating cream, and more of Mrs. Povy's sweet cakes than we ought to have. And afterwards we talked about the kindly way Arthur was treated by his parents and his brother. They all were clearly concerned over his frail health, and made sure that he sat in his usual chair near the kitchen fireplace, to keep warm against the chill of the early evening.

From that time on I became friends with Arthur and his family, and sometimes visited them on my way home from school. But things can work out strangely, and a few years after that, Mr. Povy, who was so gentle and kind with his frail little boy, proved to be an unwitting monster. Like the Angel of Death who visited ancient Egypt in the time of the Hebrews, he became an Angel of Death to those who lived in the unsuspecting village of Branford, with its sparkling stream, its tiny church, and its innocent belief that it was perfectly secure against all possible evil.

"But She Cuts Off His Head!"

My mother's long speech to my father had set me free. Not only did I now attend the Reverend Thomas Wentworth's village school, where I could start to acquire a modest education, but at home my father treated me less like a child. He even invited me, now and again, to share some of the simpler literary and scientific ideas that interested him.

His library, little by little, began to provide me with all sorts of books and pamphlets to read, some serious and some comical. He was a great lover of the theater, and owned copies of all sorts of plays—many by Shakespeare. Sometimes we read aloud together, taking turns, he assuming the men's roles and I the women's. He played Hamlet, Othello, and Oberon, while I played Ophelia, Desdemona, and Titania. What great fun it was!

Discovering how much I loved to read, my father ordered books and pamphlets for me from his bookseller in London. One pamphlet, translated from the French, I brought down to the village and shared with my friend Kate. It was all about proper conduct, and how the most highborn young noblewomen in France were expected to behave.

At one point the pamphlet writer said, "I carefully taught the princess that it was improper to take lice, or fleas, and to kill them in public, except when she was alone with members of her own family. And that it was bad manners to scratch, when one did it by habit, and not by dire necessity." After that, whenever Kate and I spied someone in the village suddenly and frantically scratching himself, we would whisper, "Not by *habit*, but by *dire necessity!*" and burst into great peals of laughter.

For my tenth birthday my father gave me a wonderful book, *The Exemplary Lives and Memorable Acts of the Nine Most Worthy Women of the World* by Thomas Heywood. All the women were very brave, and did heroic—and sometimes bloodthirsty—things to save their people and their thrones. I thought they were a grand set of ladies indeed. But it turned out that my mother had certain reservations about them, which she expressed one day to my father.

"Are these nine women," my mother said, "really suitable for young girls to read about? Take Judith—you *do* remember what she did to Holofernes?"

"I remember it very well," said my father. "But the story *is* in the Bible."

"But She Cuts Off His Head!"

"I know that it's in the Bible!" said my mother. "But she cuts off his head! Is that what Nell should be reading about?"

"My dear," said my father blandly, "I'm sure you would agree that anything in the Bible is worthy of her attention." This "orthodox" argument was so unassailable that the matter ended then and there, and I was able to carry my *Nine Worthy Women* away to safety. Later I hugged my father and thanked him for saving me from my mother's censorship. For of course, like any child, I sided first with one parent and then the other, as it suited my own aims and purposes.

Tainted Water

Sometimes when the weather was not too wet or stormy, my father would take me along to inspect his herbal gardens, where he grew all manner of strange and curious plants. These gardens were his special pride, and one day he said to me, "Although I am certainly a country squire, I do manage to practice a little medicine in my own way. I grow my various plants and, when they're ready, prepare them for your uncle John to use as medicine in his London practice. Then he informs me of the results—which plants have proved effective with some of his patients and which have not—and thus I share, however remotely, in the good work that he does in the city."

My father often was busy, too, with the rare Dutch microscope he had acquired during his exile, and now and again he would show me what he had placed under the lens. One memorable day we left the herbal gardens and came to the small leafy pond where our cattle and sheep sometimes drank, when they were in the fields. He drew a small metal flask from his pocket, knelt by the bank, and filled it with water.

"Nell—do you remember how I used to tell you and Henry that no matter how thirsty you might be, you were never, never to drink from this pond, under any circumstances?"

I said yes, I did remember, and he said, "Today I will show you why." And he led the way back to his laboratory, where he uncapped the flask and put a drop of the pond water under the microscope.

"Now look, and see what's there," he said.

I did—and shrieked with astonishment and disgust. For I saw, swimming together in the magnified drop of water, a loathsome swarm of tiny, wriggling, twitching creatures, unlike anything I had ever seen before.

"Oh, Father," I said, "what *are* these horrid things? Last month, in Branford village, a traveling preacher told the people that devils could be found everywhere—in earth, air, fire, and *water.* It all sounded rather unlikely to me, but now I wonder if these are the very sort of devils he was talking about?"

"I do not really believe so," my father said dryly. "I prefer to think that they are not supernatural beings but mere animals, and are subject to the laws of nature—as I will show you."

He picked up his flask with a pair of tongs and held it in

the flame of a candle for a considerable time. When he was satisfied, he placed another drop of the pond water under the microscope and told me to look again.

I was surprised to see that this time not a single one of the tiny creatures was stirring.

"They're quite still," I said. "They're not moving at all."

"They are dead," my father told me. "The heat has killed them. Cooked them, you might say. And that is why, Nell, if you should ever be compelled to drink water that does not come from a pure well or stream, you must be sure to boil it for no less than fifteen or twenty minutes. You will lose some of the water as steam, but the tiny animals in it will be dead, and you will not become sick from drinking it."

"Might one *die* from drinking such water?" I said.

My father frowned. "Yes, one very well might. Why do you ask me?"

I turned away from him and said, "I merely wondered." After a time I looked back. He had grown extremely pale and was staring at me intently.

"Nell, you haven't been drinking from the pond, have you? Not after all my warnings!"

I shook my head. "No, I haven't, Father. But . . ."

"But *what?*"

"Somebody else did."

There was a very long pause. Then my father said, "Did your brother?"

I nodded. "Henry told me, a few days before he fell sick. The summer afternoon had been so hot, he said, and he had been so thirsty, and the water at one end of the pond had looked so cool and pure that he drank it."

"Merciful God!" my father said.

"Might that have given him the fever?"

I thought my father would never reply. At last he said, "It might very well have given him the fever. We shall never know for certain, of course, but I think it all too likely that it did."

"Poor, foolish Henry," I said. And seeing that I was close to tears, my father took me into his arms and held me against his chest for several minutes, to comfort me.

Finally he held me away at arm's length and looked into my eyes. "This must remain a secret," he said to me. "A secret between just you and me."

I nodded, for I believed that I already understood what he was thinking.

"You mustn't tell your sister. And above all you must never tell your mother."

I nodded again.

"It would break her heart to know that such a heedless, trifling thing most probably caused Henry's death."

He took up the flask, we went outside, and he flung the contents of it into the bushes that grew by the edge of the lawn. And after that, although he and I looked many times into his microscope, we never looked again at the tainted water from the pond, nor did we ever talk about the tiny, deadly creatures that it contained.

"Pepys—Rhymes with Weeps"

As I grew a little older, I began to be included more often in the festivities when visitors came to stay with us at Branford Hall. Among such visitors were relatives and friends of my parents', traveling to and from London. There also were public officials and men of learning— physicians and teachers from the universities of Oxford and Cambridge, and from famed Gresham College in London town.

Being a child, I little appreciated or understood the importance of these scholarly guests of ours—notables like Sir Christopher Wren, Robert Boyle, and a young man of twenty years named Isaac Newton. Mr. Newton, my father told me, already showed promise of becoming the leading mathematician of the age. But he grew short of breath while climbing up with me to Eagles' Roost, and he thus struck me as a rather feeble young gallant, whether promising mathematician or no.

For the truth was I had my own way of judging our guests. If they were overall solemn, with no touch of playfulness in them, then I did not care for them much. And if they did not wish to walk about the countryside with me, or did not tell entertaining stories now and again, I liked them even less. In short, I found it difficult to esteem them highly, despite their august reputations and the importance they had in the eyes of my elders and betters.

Among our visitors from London was a singular young man whom I misjudged completely at the start—and even mispronounced his name the first time I saw it written down. I called him Mr. Samuel Peppies, until my father said, "No, Nell, his name rhymes with *weeps*—he is Mr. Samuel Pepys, and he has private business in the neighborhood, so he will be our guest for a few days. I met him in London after a lecture at Gresham College, and once or twice we supped together. He works in the government and is said to be one of the most capable and honest men in the king's service. I think you will find him quite interesting."

But I did *not* find Mr. Samuel Pepys (rhymes with weeps) quite interesting—at least not at first. In the beginning I saw only his faults. I took him for a goodnatured but overly inquisitive fool who asked everyone in the party endless questions about all manner of subjects, as if he wished to learn everything in one sitting. And so he did—but it took me a while to discover that he truly was interested in whatever he saw, tasted, touched, or heard, no matter what.

Eventually I began to alter my opinion of Mr. Pepys, and it was music that brought about the change. One morning as I was practicing on the harpsichord, I began to suspect that I was not alone, and when I'd finished the piece, I whirled around. There he was, standing behind me!

"Why, Mr. Pepys," I said, "are you then a lover of music?"

"Very much so," he replied.

"And do you play?"

"On my new recorder," he told me with a serious air. "I still do it poorly, but I shall improve my skills, as you are improving yours now."

Then, to my astonishment, he turned quite pink and said very shyly, "I also sing."

And so I found a song I could play of which he knew two verses and the chorus, and he sang them to my accompaniment. Afterwards I told him that he sang very well, which did not stray *too* far from the truth. This seemed to please him greatly, and from that morning on we became friends.

Mr. Pepys' private business dragged on, keeping him with us several extra days. During this time I learned a good deal about him, for I seemed to have the knack of drawing him out with just the right questions.

On one occasion I asked him what sort of work he did in the government. He told me how he supervised the activities of the large naval shipyard at Woolwich, outside the capital.

Another time I asked him about London. Having lived my whole life in Branford, I longed to hear everything about King Charles II, his queen, and his brother James—the Duke of York. Even more, I loved hearing about the king's spaniels—newly imported from France—which had become the current rage in fashionable circles.

Mr. Pepys spoke of his own house, which he was still finishing. He told me how pleased he was with the paintings and etchings he had started to acquire for it, along with the many books for his new library.

Then he turned pink again and said in a soft voice, "I was not born a rich man, you see, and that's why my rise in the world—though modest as yet—nevertheless fills me with great pride and pleasure."

And then, perhaps because I was a child, he confided even further in me by saying, "Do you know, Miss Eleanor, what my greatest ambition is?"

I said I couldn't guess, and he said, in the most solemn and confidential of tones, "To own a fine carriage! It is a poor boy's dream, of course—my father was, and remains, a simple tailor. But Miss Eleanor, when I do have my fine carriage one day, you must promise to visit me in London, there to ride with me across the entire city, to any and every place you choose to see!"

As he was preparing to leave Branford Hall and return home, he spoke again of London, and this time his words seemed to fill me with a dream that I had never had before. "You must come to visit our great city one day soon," he said. "And if you do, I will take you to see a hundred marvelous things!"

"What sorts of things?" I said.

"I shall take you to the palace at Whitehall, and can show you the great galleries and the Rooms of State. And you shall see the king and the Duke of York."

"And also the king's spaniels?" I said.

"I promise!"

"And then shall I ride upon the river?"

"I'll take you down the Thames," he said, "on one of the king's ships, all the way to Greenwich. And you will see the Tower of London, and the booksellers' stalls behind St. Paul's churchyard, and all manner of other grand and glorious spectacles."

"And shall I see your new house," I said, "and meet your goodwife?"

"On my honor," he told me.

"Then Mr. Pepys, to London town I shall come at the first opportunity, as soon as ever that may be."

"You will never regret it, Miss Eleanor," he said, "for in London you will see things unlike any you have ever seen in your life."

And before very long I did do just that—although neither Mr. Pepys nor I could possibly have foretold how ghastly some of those sights would be, or the awful danger in which they would place me.

Uncle John's Secret

Our most frequent visitor at Branford Hall, and the favorite of both my mother and father, was my uncle John Townley, the eminent scholar and physician, who lived in London. He was not the sort of man young children are naturally drawn to. Indeed, I believe that until I was six or seven I feared him a little and was never entirely comfortable in his presence.

Uncle John was tall and thin. He had steady gray eyes and a slow, measured way of speaking, as if each word were subjected to an intense examination before he uttered it. In company he was formal, and even with me, his own niece, there was more than a touch of formality in the way he spoke. He never called me "Nell" or "Nelly," but either "Niece Eleanor" or "Mistress Eleanor," and this from the time when I was scarcely out of the cradle.

"Yes, Niece Eleanor, that is the correct way to do it," he

would say—or more frequently, "No, Mistress Eleanor, that is quite the wrong way to deal with such a difficulty. Let me show you how to do it properly."

One summer day he encountered me as I was engaged in disposing of a quantity of our household fleas. He inquired what I had in the cloth I was carrying. I showed him the dead little pests, and he picked one up and examined it. Then another. Then a third.

"Have they all been crushed to death?" he said.

"All of them!" said I, proudly.

"By whom?"

"Me!"

"Well, Niece Eleanor, you must henceforth cease doing it. You must kill them in some other manner, without squeezing them to death between your fingers. Fleas, we believe, are not only annoying little creatures, they are a menace as well. They seem to have something evil within them—we do not yet know exactly what. But we suspect that they harbor various diseases inside their bodies. As a result, perhaps through their bites, they can pass those diseases along to people or animals who are their unwilling hosts. A dangerous creature, the flea. And so I caution you, as you value your health, to crush them no more for sport, or any other reason, but to kill them without touching them with your fingers."

On another occasion, when we were alone, the subject was not about fleas but about my father. Uncle John told me many things that never in a hundred years would my father have said about himself. "I believe, Mistress Eleanor," he said, "that you do not fully appreciate some of your father's remarkable qualities. He is generous not only to those he loves, but to those who visit his home, and to those less fortunate—many of them his tenants—who live in Branford village and its surrounding farms. He is a man of courage who attempts to conceal the fact. He has endured two years of wretched exile, the loss of his only sons, and the death of his private ambitions, and all this without a murmur of bitterness or complaint.

"But what I most admire in your father is his thirst for understanding and his openness to new ideas. During his exile he sought out an ingenious Dutchman named Anton van Leeuwenhoek, who had developed a much-improved optical instrument—a 'microscope,' to enlarge tiny objects. Your father purchased one from the man and brought it home with him—the first such instrument, as far as I know, to enter our kingdom. It is the same instrument, he tells me, that you use together now."

Then Uncle John looked around and made sure that we were still alone. Lowering his voice, he said, "Are you capable of keeping a *great* secret? You are? You are certain you can keep it?"

I swore I could, and he said, "Very well, but if you breathe even a single word of what I tell you, I shall have you publicly hanged, drawn, and quartered—do you know what that means?"

I said I did indeed, and smiled to myself, because of course I knew that his threat was merely a tease. Then Uncle John lowered his voice even further. "I don't know when it will be bestowed," he told me, "but within a year or two, I believe, your father is to receive a well-deserved honor, which I'm certain will please him enormously. He is to be elected a member of the Royal Society in London, an eminent scientific organization. However, until the time comes when I can tell your father, and invite him to London to attend the ceremony, you must not reveal one syllable of what I have told you!"

I swore again that I would be as silent as the Sphinx herself, and he said, "Mistress Eleanor, you had better be, for my entire opinion of you will depend upon your conduct in this affair!" And with these words ringing in my ears I kept his secret, you may be sure, resisting all temptation to share it with anyone else.

The Plague in Amsterdam

One afternoon my father was busy around the estate, attending to what he called, with considerable irony, "the duties of the squire." So my uncle John and I walked down to Branford village together and made a discovery there.

A peddler had arrived that day and put up a notice advertising his wares. And what a formidable host of remedies he offered to sell! Among others, there were Lozenges, Pills, Beauty Waters for the Ladies, Liquid Snuff for the Gentlemen, and Nectar and Ambrosia for those of either sex. Best of all was his Golden Elixir—a quart bottle obtainable for two shillings sixpence—which would cure almost every ill known to mankind. These included the Scurvy and Ricketts, the Kidney Stone and Gravel, Chilblains in the Hands and Feet, and Sores and

43

Swellings in the Throat, Mouth, and Gums. Not to mention the Raging Toothache, Flatulence and Other Torments in the Guts, and Worms in Every Part of the Body!

Uncle John and I went to stout John Watson's inn, at the end of the High Street, where the peddler—a shifty-eyed little man badly marked by the pox—was staying for the night. Here my uncle purchased a bottle of the Golden Elixir and carried it back to Branford Hall for examination. He concluded that it contained mostly water, a few harmless herbs and aromatic spices, and enough alcohol to make even a dying patient feel better for an hour or two.

"And that," Uncle John told me with a sigh, "is how most people in England, both the rich and the poor, are duped and swindled, and cured of nothing."

We went outside and walked through the meadow, and he sighed a second time. "But in truth," he said, "although we licensed physicians do our honest best, we possess few effective remedies. Many times we accomplish little more for the sick than do the quacksalvers and the peddler charlatans we so rightfully deplore."

We had reached my family's private chapel and the gravestones behind it. Here we paused, and Uncle John said, "Samuel and Henry—I tried to save both of your brothers, and I saved neither. That is what any physician will tell you he experiences all too frequently—failure, bitter, complete failure. The true nature of disease remains a mystery to us, and often we can do nothing for those who employ us, or for those we love."

~ ~ ~

The Plague in Amsterdam

One evening, during my uncle's next visit, we all sat together by the fireplace, and my father said, "You do seem unusually pensive tonight, John. If I were a gambler, I would wager that something unpleasant is on your mind."

"And you would win," my uncle replied with a wintry smile. "Before I left home to come up here and see you, a report arrived in London from the Netherlands."

"What report?" my mother asked.

"Last month, the worst of all possible diseases was discovered in Amsterdam. A number of cases of the Bubonic Plague."

"The Plague!" my sister, Mary, cried. "But there's been no Plague in Europe for years and years!"

"No major outbreak since 1637," said Uncle John.

"*Amsterdam*," my father murmured with a frown. "Many of our English ships sail in and out of there every week. Surely you do not believe it likely that one of them might carry the Plague back here to England?"

My uncle shrugged. "No one ever has been able to predict what course the Plague may follow. All we really know is that many times in the past, ships have carried it far and wide—beginning three hundred years ago with the Black Death. That epidemic reached Europe from the East aboard a number of merchant ships, the disease carried and spread by seagoing rats. And after the Plague arrived, as many as half the people living in Europe died within ten years' time—at least that is what the accounts that I have studied seem to say."

Seated next to Mary was the beaky-nosed scholar

she loved, the Reverend Thomas Wentworth. "You say there's been no major outbreak since 1637," he began in his high-pitched voice. "But Sir, that is almost thirty years ago. Certainly, I have heard several learned gentlemen lately say that the Plague is now a thing of the past and will never again return to Europe. Might not this 'report' of yours be a mere rumor, and nothing more?"

"It is no rumor," said Uncle John. "The Plague, in all its fury, has reappeared in Amsterdam."

"But that does not necessarily mean," my father said, "that it will reach England."

"No, it may very well not," my uncle replied, with a second smile even more wintry than the first. "And yet, my dear Richard, if *I* were a gambler, I would wager my shilling this time on the dark side of things and prepare to deal with the Plague—if and when it should arrive among us."

11

A Royal Pup

Several months later, when next my father visited London, there were fresh reports of the Plague, now raging more fiercely than ever across the waters in Amsterdam. Still, not a single case had been reported in England. And so it did seem quite possible that Uncle John had been mistaken, and that the epidemic might not reach our island shores.

My father's visits to the capital usually were brief, solitary affairs. My mother never accompanied him there. Once I asked her why. She told me that she still remembered the terror she'd felt, as a young bride in London, knowing that at any hour of the day or night the soldiers of Parliament might seize her husband and lead him away to a dark prison and death.

"Even now," she said, "my memories of London are

still so strong, Nell, that a visit there would provide me with little pleasure or diversion."

This time, when my father returned alone from London, he brought me a special gift. Not a book or pamphlet, or anything else to read, and not a lovely French lace collar, like those he brought back for my mother and Mary. But it was the most glorious gift I ever did receive as a child: a fawn-colored spaniel puppy, exactly like the new spaniel puppies King Charles himself had recently installed in his London palace.

From the first moment when the puppy leaped into my arms, I adored him madly. And after that, for many weeks, everything was bliss and contentment with me, save for one concern only: My darling had as yet no name. And so all those in our household, from the servants to several eminent guests, were permitted to express opinions on the vital question of what my puppy should be called.

Sir Christopher Wren, the famous architect, suggested "Proscenium Arch." My father assured me that he was making an "architectural" joke of some kind, which nobody else could understand. Of course, I gave Sir Christopher's notion no heed whatever.

Several days later young Isaac Newton came to stay with us, and he thought my puppy might be called "Gravitational Force," a "mathematical" joke, no doubt, to which I gave equally short shrift.

My father proposed the name Sweet Prince, in honor of Shakespeare's immortal Hamlet. But I said no, for in the play, by the time Hamlet was called Sweet Prince, he was already dead—and that would have been an ill omen for my puppy!

My mother and sister thought my pet should be called Heart's Delight, since I prized him so greatly, but I said no again. For I found this name utterly lacking in the swagger and bravado that such a handsome dog as mine truly deserved.

At last I decided that my pet was as good as the king's, and of the same breed, and since he could just as easily be living in Whitehall Palace with King Charles as with the obscure Bullens in Branford Hall, why, I decided to name him Royal. That's what I felt he was—from the tip of his cold little nose to the end of his silky, ever-wagging tail. And Mother and Mary were also right, because he *was* my heart's delight. Never in all of Christendom, I do believe, was there a happier person than I with my beloved spaniel.

Not long after Royal became a member of our household, Uncle John disclosed that my father had been elected a member of the Royal Society in London. A date in the spring had been set for the formal ceremony, at which time he would be enrolled in that august company.

I immediately reminded my uncle that I had kept his secret, and said, "Surely now you will not have me hanged, drawn, and quartered, as you threatened to do, if ever I revealed what you had told me."

And he replied, "Yes, Niece Eleanor, you have indeed kept your pledge. Therefore I will not be compelled to send you either to the public hangman at Tyburn or to the royal headsman and his sword on Tower Green."

Before long, plans began to be made for my father's London journey, and I was astonished and delighted when my mother proposed that *I* accompany him there! Mary, she said, already had visited the capital, and now I was old enough to see some of the wonders too. It was time, she said, for me to meet a new set of people, and to improve my knowledge and understanding of the polite world.

It was agreed that after my father and I reached Greater London, we would remain several days with Uncle John at his house in Westminster. Then we would travel to the other side of London and beyond, to the home of Sir John Evelyn in Deptford. There we would be his guests for a week or two, depending on the circumstances.

Sir John was an old family friend, a charter member of the Royal Society, and a wealthy, public-spirited gentleman. He was a great supporter of the Crown and each year wrote a fawning, and most tedious, poem in honor of the king's birthday. To his credit, though, he also wrote, and published at his own expense, idealistic essays on how to improve the lives of his fellow citizens. On these he expended much time and effort. Often he had been our guest at Branford Hall, and had urged any and all of the Bullens to come visit him at Sayes Court, his fine estate. Now, my mother said, was the very time to accept his invitation!

Letters of every sort were exchanged, schedules drawn

up and then revised, and clothes made ready. Finally the spring day began to draw near when I would say good-bye to familiar haunts and set off on my great adventure.

~ ~ ~

And then one evening it seemed as if all my happy prospects would be swept away. After an absence of several months, Uncle John came up from London unannounced, his manner and expression as funereal as the grave.

He wasted no time in getting to the point. "What I have feared," he said, "has now come to pass. The Plague has reached London."

"Beyond any doubt?" asked the Reverend Thomas Wentworth, who—ever eager to enjoy the company of my sister—was taking supper with us once again.

"Beyond any doubt," Uncle John replied. "The authorities have confirmed that two Frenchmen, living in the upper end of Drury Lane, died of the Plague last December. In January a number of people died of it in the parish of St. Giles. Then our weather turned severely cold, and we had much hard frost through February and early March. As a result, the Plague subsided, and most people believed that it would not return.

"They were mistaken, however. Last month we enjoyed much warmer weather, and now, in early May, the epidemic has revived. The number of deaths is increasing, and what I find most menacing of all, the Plague has spread from St. Giles to other parishes—including St. Andrews, St. Clements Dane, and Holborn."

"Then is it safe," my mother asked, "to live in London now—or to visit there?"

"If one is cautious and exercises good sense," said Uncle John, "there is absolutely no risk. Richard and Niece Eleanor will be entirely safe with me in Westminster, and also during their visit to Sir John Evelyn in Deptford. The only danger is in the infected parishes, where the Plague is established among the overcrowded poor. My guests will have no reason to be near or inside such places while they are in London.

"However," Uncle John concluded, "I determined to come here and tell you all of this anyway. I wanted you and Richard to understand how things presently stand in London, so that you can decide for yourselves what you wish to do. But as I've already said, with the exercise of prudence there really is no risk whatever in paying a visit to the capital at the present time."

And so in the end it came to nothing. My parents were satisfied that all was safe, and preparations continued to be made for our approaching journey.

~ ~ ~

As I walked through the village one afternoon with my friend Kate, we came upon the stagecoach just setting off for London town. At first the sight of it made me almost giddy with excitement. But then I began to think about *her*, and I realized with an uneasy pang that she was not going off anywhere on a great adventure, and that really I was much luckier that she in ever so many ways. This made me feel ashamed of my own good fortune, which I had done nothing to deserve but enjoyed every day of my life.

All this I tried to explain to her as we walked about. Then I suddenly burst into tears, for I felt quite wretched and knew not what else to do. But she only laughed at me and said it was all mere foolishness. For she did not envy me my London journey, Branford village being the dearest place in the world to her, and the prettiest place to see, and so why would she ever want to be anywhere else?

"However," she said, "when you *are* in London, you must remember one thing!"

"And what would that be?" I asked.

"In polite and aristocratic circles . . ."

"Yes?"

"A lady does not scratch herself by habit—but only by *dire necessity!*"

We doubled over with laughter, and by the time we'd ceased, I do believe we had become better friends than we had ever been before.

~ ~ ~

Finally the waiting was over, and the last morning came. I hugged my mother and my sister—and Royal, of course, for I was going to miss him terribly. After that we were off to Branford village, my father and I, to take our places in the London coach. We climbed inside, the doors were shut behind us, and we waved good-bye to our village friends. Then we set out on our journey to what my father always called "the greatest city in the entire civilized world."

Mr. Pepys to the Rescue

I can still remember any number of novel and surprising things that I discovered on our way to London. There were the little towns and villages where we stopped for refreshment and to stretch our legs. There was the seemingly endless royal forest that we rode past one entire morning. There were the crowded, smoky inns where we slept each night, with their tiny bedrooms and thin walls. Through these walls one heard the most intimate conversations of one's neighbors and learned the most astonishing facts about their private lives! And there was the coach itself in which we rode. It was a cold, cramped torture chamber, apparently built without any of the springs that might have eased our sufferings as we jarred and jolted our way along several rutted highways toward our destination.

But all of these impressions were swept aside when we

reached journey's end. There was so much to see in the late-afternoon sunlight—a grand panorama of people, houses, the famous River Thames, churches, bridges, market stalls, carriages, carts, horses, dogs, pigs, chickens, cats, pigeons, and every other manner of domestic fowl and animal. And then still more houses. Some tall and noble, some low, mean, and crowded together. And still more churches, and market stalls, and shops, and people—until I realized the paintings and drawings I'd previously seen of London had ill prepared me for the place itself. It was then I began to believe that at least half of mankind made its residence in our British capital.

Our journey from Branford to London had been a most tiring one. And so that first evening, although I would have enjoyed seeing my father honored by the Royal Society, I was just as happy to be excluded from the ceremony because of my youth. Indeed, I felt most grateful to Uncle John's housekeeper, Mrs. Hamilton. She provided me with a delicious meat pie for supper, and then, a wonderful tubful of hot water and rose petals in which I bathed before retiring to bed. There I slept "the sleep of the just"—or of the exhausted—and did not awaken until well after dawn.

For the next four or five days, my father was my London guide. He showed me some of the churches that Sir Christopher Wren had designed, as well as the buildings of Gresham College and the Guildhall. One afternoon he took me to Gray's Inn Walks. There he showed me the very spot where he had met my mother, and she had won his heart.

I stood exactly where she had stood. "Oh, Father," I said, "this is lovely! It's where our family began."

"Yes, Nell, it all began here. I felt sure you'd want to visit this place."

Sometimes my father and I rode in Uncle John's carriage and sometimes in a hired coach. But however we traveled, and wherever we went, we always seemed to encounter crowds of Londoners—such crowds that my innocent country eyes scarcely could credit the numbers of people they beheld.

And always we were extremely careful to avoid the Plague-infested parts of the city, which now had become more numerous and more dangerous. For as Uncle John informed us, during the past week or two the death rate in several poor London parishes had climbed alarmingly. As a result, he said, the day might well be approaching when the danger would become so great that people of means would decide to abandon the city and retire to the safety of the countryside.

Believing ourselves to be entirely safe, however, my father and I dined out several times at the homes of friends and relatives, including my uncle George, who ran a girls' school in London. On these occasions I practiced my best company manners, took careful note of what the ladies were wearing, and tried to observe how polite London society behaved.

Then one afternoon a message arrived from Branford Hall with the most doleful news. Some of our domestic animals had fallen sick, our bailiff was at his wits' end, and my father's presence at home was required as soon as

possible. Clearly his holiday was over—and as a consequence, it seemed that my own holiday was over as well.
He would have to leave for Branford Hall on the next
morning's coach, and I would have to accompany him.
There would be no chance to see any more of London, or
of visiting Sir John Evelyn and his family in Deptford.

I made no effort to conceal my disappointment and
played quite shamelessly, I fear, on my uncle's sympathies,
for I desperately needed him as an ally in this affair. And
apparently my dramatic efforts were successful, for almost at once he intervened on my behalf.

"Of course, Richard," he said to my father, "you must
set off for Branford at once and see to your domestic con-
cerns. But Mistress Eleanor can perfectly well remain
here with me until she goes on to visit Sir John at Sayes
Court. And then, once you've settled your difficulties at
home, you can rejoin her there, and afterwards return together to Branford Hall as you'd originally planned."

My father was unconvinced. "But what will she do in
London without me?" he said. "*You're* too busy to look after her, John, so she'll have no one to take her about.
She'll just sit in your house to no good purpose, the time
will be ill spent, and all at a great inconvenience to you
and your household. No, I think that Nell had best accept
her disappointment and come home with me tomorrow."

And then—quite providentially, it seemed to me—a
visitor was announced. A gentleman named Samuel Pepys.
The very same Mr. Pepys who once had solemnly promised
to escort me about and show me all the finest sights in
London, if ever I came to the capital.

This he pledged to do now, after he had been made to understand my unhappy predicament. And so everything was quickly arranged. My father left for home the following morning, and I was entrusted to the daily escort service of that rising public official, amateur musician, and recently elected member of the Royal Society, Mr. Samuel Pepys of 5 Axe Yard, London.

Of Guardians and Queens

Mr. Pepys had not yet acquired his own carriage, but there was no shortage of hackneys for hire. So without any difficulty, he and I, accompanied by his goodwife, Elizabeth, traveled everywhere around London, exactly as he had promised.

Mrs. Pepys, I discovered, was a Frenchwoman—an amiable person, I thought, but with a vaguely unhappy air, as though some secret trouble constantly vexed her.

When I said as much one night to Uncle John, he pursed his lips thoughtfully and then said, "I should imagine, Mistress Eleanor, that you are right. It is said in certain quarters that young Mr. Pepys has a considerable interest in the ladies, and that is something which invariably causes a wife much vexation of spirit. And that also is why I arranged for Mrs. Pepys to bear you company on your London excursions, and to act as your guardian."

"My guardian?" I cried.

"Your guardian!" said Uncle John firmly.

I must have colored mightily then, and probably gasped as well. "But Uncle John," I finally said, "I am scarcely more than a dozen years of age! I am not yet a woman certainly—and so what could you have been thinking?"

There was an extended silence from Uncle John before he replied. "Niece Eleanor, I was thinking that while it is true you are not yet a woman, it is equally true that you are teetering on the very edge of becoming one. And moreover, that you are reasonably pretty, as such things go. Considering my young friend Pepys' reputation with the ladies, I concluded that a guardian was what you would require, a guardian was what you would have, and my friend Pepys should be put on notice that I had my eye on him in regard to you and your London holiday."

So I learned for the first time that my appearance was putting a new set of thoughts into some people's minds, and that some people deemed me pretty enough, "as such things go." Yet all this seemed quite foolish the next morning, when I rejoined Mr. Pepys and his wife. For it was perfectly clear that he had no wish to flirt with me, or any such ridiculous thing, though it was very sweet of Uncle John to have been so concerned with my safety and welfare.

With no flirtatious nonsense, then, to impede our good times, Samuel and Elizabeth Pepys and I toured London for the next several days and saw all manner of interesting things. We visited Whitehall Palace, and there at a distance, in the Privy Garden, I observed the king himself strolling about with numerous courtiers and ladies. He was a tall young man whose features I took to be rather weak and self-indulgent, although perhaps I already knew of his character from my father.

Neither the king's brother, the Duke of York, nor the queen were present that day. To my delight, however, the king's spaniels made an appearance. Although they possessed some charm, I judged them to be not nearly so handsome as my own dear Royal—whom I hadn't had the time to think about for several days but suddenly missed most terribly!

Soon Mr. Pepys was called away for a few minutes on business, and during his absence Mrs. Pepys opened my eyes to some of the extravagance of the Royal Court. Being a Frenchwoman, she knew much about taste and style. She pointed out how over-elaborate the ladies' costumes were, and how idle and foppish the gentlemen looked in their long coats, which hung down as far as their knees. It was a new style, she told me, recently introduced by the king, which all the courtiers had slavishly adopted the very moment they'd seen His Majesty dressed that way!

One afternoon Mr. Pepys was obliged to attend a meeting at his office. It soon began to rain heavily, so Mrs. Pepys and I decided to remain indoors at their house.

After a time we retired to her chambers. There she asked me if I'd be interested in seeing some of her cosmetic devices, for such things were very popular with the ladies of London.

I said I'd be most interested indeed, and she had me sit

at her dressing table, where she placed a looking glass in my hand. "Now, Nell," she said, "what do you see?"

I looked and then replied, "I see myself—much as usual."

She laughed and said, "No, you see a young lady with rich chestnut hair, clear dark eyes, and fair skin with nary a wrinkle in it."

"But I'm much too young to have wrinkles," I said.

She laughed once more and replied, "That's what we all think—in the beginning." Then she showed me some of her supplies, and I was amazed at the assortment she'd acquired.

To keep her skin from aging, she used both orange-flower water and apricot cream. She had several dark crayons to color her lips, though the color soon blurred and faded, she told me. And for formal occasions she had a blue crayon to color her upper eyelids.

However, she no longer used ceruse, a mixture containing white lead that many women employed to cover skin blemishes. Mrs. Pepys said she wondered if lead might not cause bodily harm, and so she now avoided it.

But she did confess that her sparse eyebrows and excess facial hair were an extreme annoyance, and for each she had a remedy that appalled me. Sometimes when attending a party, she wore two pretty, false eyebrows, which she stuck on and hoped would not drop off before she got home. She showed me a pair of these and told me they'd been made out of mouse skin!

Worse still was the much-recommended mixture she used for removing excess hair. It was made of vinegar and cat dung, and when she told me, I said to myself, "Now that is truly disgustful! I do believe I'd rather have a beard!"

One evening Uncle John and I dined with Mr. and Mrs. Pepys in their handsomely furnished house. And what a night it was! Mr. Pepys took such evident pride in being our host. He pointed out the fine pictures on the walls and the pretty blue Dutch tiles around the fireplace, and then he offered us a banquet that would have done Whitehall itself proud!

Afterwards I wrote down and memorized the various dishes we had been served: a small eel pie; a dish of marrowbones; two chickens, cooked together in a savory sauce with a dozen larks (it was delicious, cooked according to a rare French recipe of Mrs. Pepys' late mother); then caviar, taken from a huge sturgeon caught in the Thames that very morning—the caviar all properly mashed up, and most fresh and succulent; and finally, three different cheeses to sample—one from Holland, one from France, and a fine English Stilton, which I much preferred.

Once dinner was over, we retired to another chamber, and there, each of us drank a marvelous posset—hot, sweetened milk, curdled with wine, of course. I was seldom allowed to have it at Branford Hall, and now it made me feel both a trifle giddy and very grown up indeed.

But of all the things I saw and did during my holiday, I remember best the visit I paid, accompanied by Mr. and Mrs. Pepys, to the famous Tower of London. I had never been inside a castle before, and was surprised to find it so solemn and dismal, with its thick stone battlements above and its grim, dark, menacing dungeons far below.

Toward the end of our visit we came upon a tiny bit of grassy meadow within the walls. Here, Mr. Pepys informed us, was the place of execution for royal and noble prisoners who had been condemned to death.

"And this is the nineteenth of May!" he announced. "The anniversary of a famous execution!"

"*Whose* execution?" Mrs. Pepys asked in a wary voice.

"Of a beautiful queen, my dear, who greatly displeased her husband—of Henry VIII's wife Anne Boleyn!"

And so I found myself standing where once had stood my ill-fated distant relative! And this on the very day of the year when she had died! She had stood there, I knew, at the foot of the scaffold, believing to the end that her vengeful husband would take pity on her and relent. That he would issue a last-minute pardon and spare her life. But—cold and remorseless man—he had wickedly deceived her into thinking there was hope when hope there was none. He'd never had any intention of pardoning her. And so no last-minute reprieve had come, and there had been no mercy. She had mounted the scaffold bravely, knelt silently and without protest, and bared her lovely, delicate neck to the executioner's cruel sword. . . .

"Child—you are looking extremely pale!" I heard Mrs. Pepys exclaim. "This is an unhappy place!" And she took me by the hand and led us all away. I'm sure there were tears in my eyes as we left that tragic scene, where a proud and misfortunate woman—and my own remote ancestor—had ended her life with such unparalleled courage and feminine serenity!

14
A Marriage Proposal

Mr. Pepys had official business in Deptford, near Sir John Evelyn's home. Thus he offered to escort me there aboard one of the riverboats that he regularly traveled in. My uncle John gave his approval to the plan, for by then he realized that Mr. Pepys had no designs on my youthful person and that I could be entrusted to his care without a guardian.

It was cold and stormy the morning we left London. When we reached the Thames wharf, we could see white-caps on the water, for the wind was blustering mightily, and swirling everywhere.

I had never been on the water before and soon made an unwelcome discovery—I was a very poor sailor indeed! Five minutes aboard our tossing galley and I felt grievously ill. Five minutes after that and I was lying on the rude mattress that Mr. Pepys had provided me with in this emergency. My recent breakfast had been violently launched into the deep, my brow was soaked with sweat, and there was a fervent wish in my heart that the Good Lord take pity on me and allow me to die!

But the waves did somewhat subside during the last few miles of our passage. Once we were back onshore, I quickly recovered my spirits, so by the time we reached Sayes Court, I'd changed my mind and decided to live yet awhile longer.

I spent a month at Sayes Court with Sir John Evelyn, his wife, Mary, and their young son, who also was named John. It was an idyllic month, during which I was instructed in any number of interesting subjects by my learned host and was made to feel all but a member of that generous and amiable family.

In addition to being a founder of the Royal Society, Sir John was an ardent supporter of the Crown, and a gentleman of wide knowledge and attainments. One day he showed me his miniature paintings; another day it was a wonderful handmade book of dried leaves, marvelously preserved with their natural colors; on a third day he let me read a rare and ancient letter written by Mary, Queen of Scots, and a reply, written by Queen Elizabeth of England—daughter of the tragic Anne Boleyn!

My host also was a great student of landscape architecture, and Sayes Court was widely admired for its trees and gardens, and for the unusual beauty of its spacious grounds. And of course he was a most public-spirited man, who wished to improve the daily lives of his fellow citizens, especially those who lived in London. To this purpose he had written a little book several years before, called *Fumifugium, or the Smoke of London Dissipated*, which he read aloud to me one afternoon. When I praised him for it, he seemed pleased, in the way of most authors.

Sir John's wife, Mary, was a sweet-tempered woman who, like my own mother, had suffered much over the early deaths of her children. Little John was the sole survivor of six sons. On learning this, I told her of my two dead brothers, especially of my dear friend Henry. She hugged me and sighed, and said she felt most grateful to God that her son John was well and thriving, and imagined that my mother felt the same about my sister and me.

John was a studious boy, greatly resembling his father, and already a considerable scholar in Greek and Latin. We quickly became friends and spent much time together. But I was ill prepared for what he said to me one afternoon as we stood near the pond, admiring some of the recently planted elm trees.

"Nell," he said to me with a most serious air, "I know that you will be leaving soon, and I have something to declare to you before you depart."

"What do you wish to declare to me?" I asked him.

His manner became truly grave. Gazing up into my eyes, he said, "Nell, I love you most sincerely, and wish to marry you as soon as ever I am old enough to do so!"

My suitor was nine or ten years old, and most earnest in the matter, as I could see, and of course I would not have hurt his feelings for anything in the world.

So I looked equally grave, and replied, "I am much

honored by your declaration, and thank you for it. But dear John, I must point out that in a few years' time, when you are ready to marry, well, by then *I* shall be almost an old lady! I shall probably have lost whatever pretty looks I may have now—as such things go. After those eight or ten years have passed, why, you would find me plain and ugly, and would want someone younger and more suitable to your tastes. So I think we should not pledge ourselves now, but if you are willing, we should agree to be friends in the meantime, until the matter can be discussed again, when we both are old enough."

He thought all of this over and finally said, "Very well, I will wait and ask for your pledge at some future time. But ask again I shall, for you have won my heart forever!"

I thanked him once more, and gave him a kiss on the cheek to soothe his impatience and disappointment. And so I would leave Sayes Court with the first marriage proposal I had ever received. And to tell the truth of it, although my suitor was but a mere child, nevertheless I found the matter curiously gratifying.

Lord and Lady Brockton

Toward the end of my visit to Sayes Court the question began to be asked: Who would accompany me on my return to London? My father was still back in Branford, dealing with the disease that was ravaging our domestic animals, and so he could not come and fetch me. Mr. Pepys was not available to escort me, for he was busy in London, performing his duties at the Naval Office. And my uncle John had to remain in Westminster because his most valued patient—a duke, no less!—was painfully ill with the gout, and expected his physician to dance attendance on him morning and night.

As the days passed, the question became more urgent. A letter from my uncle spoke of the rapid changes that were taking place in the capital. With the advent of extremely hot weather, the Plague had begun to spread alarmingly, invading many previously unaffected parishes and claiming an increasing number of lives. So bad had things become that one day King Charles and his court had abruptly fled from the city to distant Oxford. More and more of the town's leading citizens were also packing up their household possessions and escaping into the countryside. Clearly, it was time for Mistress Eleanor to leave Deptford and return to Westminster while it was still safe to do so, and following that, to return home to Branford at the earliest possible date.

My host, Sir John, then generously volunteered to see me back to Westminster himself, and so the question seemed settled at last. But only a day or two later he was unexpectedly ordered away to Dover, there to perform his duties as a Royal Commissioner in charge of the many Dutch prisoners-of-war lately captured at sea. Sir John then made ready to depart, and I was left once more without an escort.

At this point Lord Brockton came to my rescue. He was a wealthy man and one of the most fervent Royalists in the county. A neighbor of the Evelyns, he was known—at least by reputation—to my parents and my uncle John.

Lord Brockton and his wife were planning to leave shortly for London. After sailing up the Thames, they would be met by their own carriage—and I would accompany them on their journey. Because of the Plague they intended to remain in the capital only a single night before moving on to Oxford. Since their London inn was on the outskirts of Westminster, it would be but a trifling inconvenience for them to leave me off at my uncle's house.

A perfect plan—or so it seemed when Sir John and Lady Mary first suggested it.

Once aboard our small river craft, I began to make the acquaintance of my benefactors. Lord Brockton was a portly, florid, middle-aged gentleman, endowed with a generous supply of good manners, but with what I soon came to suspect was a deficiency of good sense. His young wife was beautiful, selfish, and half his age. It took but a few minutes of our voyage before I realized that he was utterly besotted with her charms, and completely under her feminine domination.

No seat in our modest vessel was to her satisfaction, and so to make her more comfortable, I was obliged to exchange places with her at least three or four times. The food we had brought along for our luncheon was too coarse for her delicate taste, until I declared a piece of cheddar most excellent. She then gently but firmly appropriated the remainder of the cheese for herself. And all the while her doting husband hovered about her, the most obedient of slaves.

But finally, as the sun set and the long evening twilight began, we reached our destination. Crossing one of the city's wharves, we took our places in Lord Brockton's heavy gilded carriage. Amid Lady Brockton's innumerable trunks and boxes we set out on our passage across the city to Westminster.

Almost at once I realized how much the city had changed since first I had seen it, on my arrival from Branford two months before. There were still considerable numbers of people in the main thoroughfares, but the small, narrow streets that intersected them were nearly deserted. Where had the bustling crowds gone to? I wondered. Could so many have died or fallen sick that the streets were empty now? Or were people reluctant to leave their homes for fear of catching the Plague from those already infected?

And then, in the gathering dusk, we came upon a startling sight—Londoners, in full panic, fleeing the city! Evidently they were the day's stragglers, and were hurrying themselves along as best they could in order to reach the countryside before dark. There were carts and wagons heaped high with clothing, furniture, and bedding; there were women and children riding aloft, and men walking beside the horses; and often the children were holding household pets—cats and dogs, pigeons and parrots, and a single black crow, like an omen of death, glaring out of a huge wire cage.

These carts and wagons so clogged the main thoroughfares that at times we scarcely moved at all, and finally Lady Brockton became impatient. She had no desire, she said, to spend the entire evening in her carriage. Soon, in order to hasten our progress, she persuaded her husband that we should leave the Strand and take to the less-traveled backstreets.

It was a grave error. Our elderly coachman flicked his whip, and now turning left and now right, we began to jolt our way through a maze of dim, mean, narrow streets.

Suddenly we struck a deep rut in the road. Our carriage

lurched forward, swayed back and forth, and came to rest at a precarious angle, the horses half out of their shafts and quite mad with fear and confusion. Extricating ourselves from the carriage, we could see that one of the wheels had all but broken off its axle and was in great need of repair.

It was growing darker, and we were stranded in a deserted lane in an unfamiliar part of town. I felt a rush of fear—but in this I was alone. Our coachman was calm, his sole concern the welfare of his horses. Lord Brockton, as always, was well-meaning and fuddled, while Lady Brockton remained as cool as ice and—unfortunately—in command of her husband. She thought of what to do next, and once again it was a grave error.

Her plan was this: She would stay behind with the carriage and the coachman, who was armed with a pistol, ready to provide protection, should any of the inhabitants of the immediate neighborhood emerge from their homes and threaten to make difficulties. Meanwhile, Lord Brockton and I would walk to the nearest thoroughfare and there hire a hackney coach, in which we would speedily return to rescue Lady Brockton and her possessions.

However, neither she nor her husband nor I had the slightest idea where the nearest thoroughfare *was.* No matter, she said; the coachman knew the streets of the city, because it was his business to do so, and therefore, before we departed on our quest, he would instruct us how to proceed.

Unhappily, the coachman was not a native of London

and had seldom driven the gilded Brockton carriage around the city. But he was unwilling to remind her of this—for what reason, I never did learn—and blithely gave us a series of worthless instructions.

And so Lord Brockton and I set off into the dark unknown, not realizing that we were about to enter one of the poorest parishes in the city, where the Plague had been raging unchecked for the better part of two deadly months.

The Death Cart

For a brief while we walked uneasily through the fading twilight, now turning down one dismal, squalid lane and then another, as we sought to make our way to the nearest thoroughfare. Little by little the houses became more ramshackle and disorderly, the air more stifling and malodorous. Here and there, among the shadows, a few dim, wraith-like figures drifted about, silently, warily, no one pausing to exchange a greeting or to converse with his neighbor.

Suddenly Lord Brockton stopped and seized my arm. "That house over there!" he said. "There's a red cross painted on the door! Do you know what that means?"

I knew all too well, for Uncle John had spoken of the red cross many times.

"It means the Plague is inside that house," I said. "The constables have shut it up to prevent people from entering, and to keep the sick who are inside from coming out and infecting others."

"And look—there's another one with a cross!" Lord Brockton said. "And a third!"

We started forward again, and by the time we'd reached the end of the narrow lane, we had passed four more houses with the foot-high red crosses on the front doors, and the words "Lord have mercy upon us" inscribed close above.

"Seven!" my companion said. "What a Plague spot we have stumbled into, Miss Bullen!"

In front of us was a small parish church. An elderly clergyman, white-haired and gaunt, was standing on the front steps. We approached and explained our predicament. In a most kindly manner, he said that as soon as ever he was able, he would show us the way to the nearest thoroughfare, where surely we could find a hackney coach.

We asked what parish we were in, and when he replied, "St. Giles," I remembered what Uncle John had said about it, and again my heart contracted with fear. For I knew that we had come to one of the most hazardous parts of London. To a neighborhood where the Plague had been raging since the spring, and where week after week countless victims had sickened and died.

The clergyman, the Reverend Robert Frith, then told us that he was waiting for The Cart to arrive, and as the hour was growing late, it would not be long before it came. Neither Lord Brockton nor I had the wit to ask what particular cart he was awaiting, and so we were totally unprepared when the cart in question finally did appear.

It was the Death Cart for the parish of St. Giles. A large, rickety wooden vehicle, filled to the very top with its tragic load of Plague victims.

I was too stunned by what I saw to cry out or even to make a sound. There were at least twenty-five or thirty dead people in the cart, men and women, young and old, and among them several children too. Some were fully clothed, as though they had expired in the street. Some were in their nightclothes, and two or three had nightcaps on their heads. Some wore nothing but their shirts or shifts, and some were entirely naked—all pitched onto the cart in whatever condition they had been found and, at day's end, brought to the churchyard for burial.

Behind the cart came a bedraggled band of mourners. Some were silent and some were weeping, and one poor, demented woman kept crying, "Alice! Alice!" for her dead child. All were following their loved ones on their journey to the grave. It was a common grave, the Reverend Robert Frith explained to us, for so many already had died in the parish, and so many more were sick and dying now, that there were scarcely any able-bodied gravediggers left. And so each evening the latest victims were placed together in a common grave, and a brief prayer was said for their souls.

We entered the graveyard beyond the church, and when I beheld the deep, awful pit in the earth, and the cart beginning to be emptied into it, I shut my eyes. I did not open them again until I heard the clergyman's benediction, and a murmuring of "Amens" from the mourners.

Behind me, I heard the demented woman cry, "Alice!" once more. I turned, and there she was, not three feet away, staring at me. A miserable despairing creature, driven mad by her grief.

"Alice, you're alive!" she cried, and in a moment of pure horror, I realized she believed that *I* was her daughter, and that Alice had not died of the Plague after all!

Before I could move, she was upon me. Her breath was foul, her hair filthy and uncombed, her eyes wild. She seized me around the waist and, crying out, "Alice!" one last time, began to shower me with frantic kisses. She had an open, running sore on her forehead and another on her nose, and I was sure that she carried the Plague, and that I would catch the disease from her and die.

Lord Brockton, of course, remained paralyzed with confusion and was no help whatever. But the Reverend Robert Frith came to my aid, pulled the madwoman away, and did his utmost to calm and soothe my feelings. He soon led us off and in a few minutes helped us to reach the nearest thoroughfare, where we quickly found a hackney coach for hire.

I did not see Lady Brockton again that night. We were now near Westminster, and when I said to Lord Brockton, "Please take me to my uncle's house at once!" he obeyed me as though I'd been his wife. Within a few minutes we were knocking on my uncle's door.

His housekeeper, Mrs. Hamilton, greeted us, and I threw myself into her arms. A moment later my uncle appeared. Our tale was quickly told, and our belated arrival explained, but not a word of it pleased my uncle John in the least.

He was, as I now came to realize, a different Uncle John—one whom I had never seen before. He was in a rage—so angry that I thought, from his fiery cheeks and his glowing eyes, that he might strike Lord Brockton with his fist.

"You infernal imbecile!" he shouted. "How could you have been foolish enough to leave the main street and go tearing off blindly into the back alleys of London? How could you have gotten to St. Giles, the one place above all others to avoid in the city, and there to endanger my niece's life? You should be hanged on the gallows for your ignorance, or whipped for your criminal stupidity!"

Lord Brockton then was sent away in disgrace. I later learned that he rescued Lady Brockton and her possessions, and that the next day they fled to Oxford and there joined the king and his Royal Court.

For myself, Uncle John immediately gave Mrs. Hamilton her instructions, and all possible measures began to be taken to preserve my health. The clothes I had worn that day were confiscated, and I was soon immersed in a tubful of hot water and thoroughly scrubbed. Afterwards my hair was even more thoroughly scrubbed in a large pewter basin by Mrs. Hamilton.

Uncle John prescribed a sleeping draft, which I swallowed down, and I was already in my bed and drowsing when he appeared.

"I shall die of the Plague, shall I not?" I asked him.

"I hardly think that likely," he replied. "Mrs. Hamilton did not find a single flea in your clothing, nor any in your hair. And she has informed me that there were no marks of any flea bites on your skin. So I believe that you have escaped unscathed from your ill-conceived expedition to St. Giles, and your unhappy encounter with the madwoman there."

"But I'm certain she carried the Plague!" I said. "I saw that she had two running sores on her face!"

"Such sores have nothing to do with the Plague," said Uncle John. "Nor do I think that people catch the Plague directly from one another through casual contacts, except very rarely, despite what the general public believes. However, such sores have everything to do with the *scrofula*, or what is commonly called 'the king's evil.' Fortunately though—because of the prompt measures we have taken tonight—I think it most unlikely that you will contract either of these two diseases, despite the hazards you have run today."

He drew a chair up to the side of my bed and took my small hand between both of his large ones.

"I failed your two brothers in the past," he said, "but now, the good Lord willing, I shall not fail you."

Then he smiled, as he so rarely did, and said, "Mistress Eleanor, you have indeed been in considerable danger today, but there is every reason to suppose that you have passed through it without harm. Time alone will prove the case, but I do think that all will be well."

And I closed my eyes, for the sleeping draft was strong, and slept the deepest sleep I had ever known.

Uncle John at Branford Hall

After that single evening in St. Giles, I was a changed person. Gone was the carefree child who had come to London two months before, so wide-eyed and expectant, so eager to see and experience every new thing. In her place there now was a more thoughtful and wary creature, who had come to realize how many more uncertainties and dangers there were in the world than ever she had previously suspected.

Despite my uncle's reassuring words, a fear of dying of the Plague continued to haunt me. At night my dreams were filled with awful visions—of the St. Giles Death Cart, of the burial pit behind the church, of the madwoman raining wet, loathsome kisses on my cheeks, my forehead, my half-averted lips.

For ten anxious days I remained in Westminster while Uncle John's noble and eminent patients, one by one, packed up their possessions, shut up their houses, and left the Plague-ravaged city for the safety of the countryside.

Finally, with no more patients to attend, my uncle decided it was time to shut up his own house. He hired two watchmen to guard it during his absence. Then he sent Mrs. Hamilton away to her north-country relatives, and early one morning carried me off in his carriage, back to Branford Hall.

I remember almost nothing about our journey, save only that I was mildly feverish during most of the daylight hours and slept fitfully during much of the nighttime. As soon as we reached home, Mother put me to bed. For the next week or two I was thoroughly indisposed, having little interest or regard for anything except sleeping, and that for hours and hours at a time.

Slowly, though, my appetite began to increase; I grew more active and alert, and a little more like my former self. Because I had not developed any symptoms of the Plague or the king's evil, Uncle John declared that I need no longer fear succumbing to either one. Yet even many weeks after my return home, I still experienced sudden spells of melancholy, and my dreams continued to be haunted by St. Giles and what I had seen there.

~ ~ ~

Uncle John did not go back to live in London that summer, but remained with us at Branford Hall as a permanent guest. It would have been foolish of him to have done otherwise. By then the Plague was devastating all sections of the capital, including Westminster, and he would have been risking his life to no purpose had he returned there. Each day additional hundreds were dying in the city, and though all sorts of people were making wild claims that they could save you from the Plague, their claims were universally false. No physician, surgeon, apothecary, medical quack, preacher, *or* astrologer really could guarantee that anyone who followed his advice would escape the dread disease. And as the summer heat in the capital increased week by week, the Plague grew ever more contagious and deadly.

Stranded with us in the country, and having no other patients to attend, Uncle John began to take an even greater interest in my own case. Before long he insisted on a change in my routine. Ever since my return, Royal, my beloved pet, had been decreed a nuisance and banished from my presence. Now, my uncle said, his banishment was to end.

"The spaniel is your proper charge," he said to me one morning, "and you must begin to care for him again as you did formerly—commencing today!"

And so I did, and as my physician had anticipated, I soon was thinking less about myself and more about my darling spaniel. Within a few days my sleep grew less troubled, and my spirits finally became more cheerful and buoyant again.

~ ~ ~

One afternoon my mother said to me, "Both you and I have had our misfortunes in London, haven't we? I wonder, Nell, whether you'll want to return there someday, as your father does. Or whether, like me, you'll never care to see the place again."

Thinking only of St. Giles, I burst out, "Oh, I *never* want to visit London again!"

But then I remembered the rest of my visit, and the many delightful and diverting things I had seen and done there.

"No, Mother, that isn't so," I said a moment later. "I shall certainly want to visit there again—but not when the Plague is everywhere and so many people are suffering and dying."

My mother thought for a while, looked at me with some degree of care, and finally said, "Yes, I'm sure you will go back to London one day. Perhaps merely for diversion, or perhaps to find a husband."

"A husband?" said I.

"There will not be very many choices for you here in Branford," she said, shaking her head. "Ah, yes, Nell, the time is not *that* far away when such things will have to be considered."

And suddenly I felt less like a child than I ever had before, and enormously pleased that my mother regarded me in this new and flattering light.

Mr. Povy and the Plague

Most days that summer my uncle John was with us at Branford Hall, but he did have several friends who lived in other parts of the county, and so, now and again, he would be away, visiting their homes. He was away one early evening when the Reverend Thomas Wentworth came to us for supper.

By then the beaky-nosed scholar and my sister were officially betrothed, and his presence at Branford Hall had become even more constant. On this occasion he reported that Mr. Povy, Branford's highly skilled tailor, had fallen sick and was being treated by Mr. Ford, the village apothecary.

"Mr. Ford has become somewhat uneasy about his patient," the minister said, helping himself to another morsel of boiled mutton and beginning to chew on it reflectively. "Mr. Povy has a low fever and a rather persistent cough. Neither one has responded to the apothecary's remedies. And so this afternoon Mr. Ford came to me at the rectory. He told me that he would not take it amiss if your brother"—here nodding politely to my mother—"the famous London physician, Dr. Townley, were to examine his patient and see what additional remedies might be tried."

The next afternoon I saw Uncle John come riding up the lane to the Hall. I ran outside and told him about Mr. Povy being sick, and what Thomas Wentworth had said. My uncle gathered up some of his instruments, and then the two of us walked down to the village. There I left him at the apothecary's and went on to the rectory to find Kate.

It was a lovely afternoon, the sky almost cloudless, the air sweet and mild—a perfect day to amble everywhere in idleness and pleasure. This Kate and I did for an hour or so, greeting at every turn those villagers who had decided to come out-of-doors and enjoy the glorious weather.

In later times I would remember some of those we met that afternoon—portly Mrs. Ford, the apothecary's wife, marching along the High Street with a basket of leeks under her arm; that old, red-faced villain Captain Dunstan, trudging back toward his house, a jug of spirits gripped tightly in his gnarled hand, and his son, "Pinching Will," shuffling along at his side; stout John Watson standing on the steps of his inn, smoking a pipe and joking with wiry Oliver Robinson, the village cobbler, who suddenly began to dance about and curse because a wasp had stung him on the wrist. And then there was Mrs. Povy outside her husband's tailor shop, instructing their son Jasper on the errand he was to run; and Andrew Goodfellow, Branford's amiable and muscular blacksmith, blowing up his fire with a bellows, and letting Kate and me have a turn at blowing it up too. An ordinary village afternoon, not so very different from many others—yet one that would linger in my memory forever afterwards.

When Kate and I finally met my uncle in front of the apothecary's, he said not a word about Mr. Povy, but instead sent my friend off to the rectory with a message: Dr. Wentworth would be particularly welcome at Branford Hall that evening. Supper would be delayed, if necessary, until he arrived. It was a matter of some urgency—Kate would not forget, would she! She would be sure to relate the message to her uncle, would she not!

Then Uncle John and I returned home, neither of us speaking more than a word or two the entire way. My head was buzzing with questions, but his sober and pensive expression kept me from asking them.

In good time our minister arrived at Branford Hall, and the six of us—he and my sister, Mary; my mother and father; and my uncle and I—all sat down to supper. When the servants had retired to the kitchen, the rest of us fell silent and looked at Uncle John.

He cleared his throat and said, "What I am about to tell you must not be repeated—at least not for the present. I have thoroughly examined Mr. Povy now, and have spoken with him at considerable length. I am not absolutely certain, because his symptoms have not yet developed fully, as I anticipate they will—by tomorrow, or certainly by the day after. Nevertheless, I have concluded that it is almost certain the village tailor has contracted the Plague. He is grievously ill. He and others too, I fear, are almost surely going to die."

The Beaky-Nosed Scholar

At first none of us broke the silence that followed my uncle's words. The idea that poor Mr. Povy might be dying, and that others probably were fated to die as well, left us stunned and mute.

Finally, when my father did speak, it was to ask a question that had not even occurred to me. "John," he said, "where do you imagine Mr. Povy caught the disease? Has he recently been to London? Or to Bristol, or one of our other ports? Because those are the only places in the kingdom, so I've been told, where the Plague has appeared."

My uncle shook his head. "Mr. Povy has been neither to London nor to anywhere else. I have talked with Mrs. Povy concerning that subject, and she has informed me that her husband has not been a half mile outside Branford—not once—during the past three years."

"Then surely," my mother said, "the unfortunate man has caught the Plague from a traveler. Someone who passed through Branford village. Someone who must have stopped at the inn before resuming his journey."

Uncle John shook his head a second time. "I believe that is not very likely," he said. "Mr. Povy has always been a homebody who spent most of his time either working in his shop or enjoying himself in front of his kitchen fire. And I suspect it was in his own workshop that he caught the Plague—I mean to learn if that is so, before very much longer."

Thus far Thomas Wentworth, quite uncharacteristically, had been silent. Now when he spoke, his words sobered the rest of us even further. And as I looked across the table at him, I had the uncanny feeling that he was undergoing some mysterious kind of change.

"Dr. Townley," he said, "how many of the villagers do you think are going to die?"

Uncle John did not reply at first. He took a sip of wine, swallowed it, pursed his lips, and stared wordlessly back at Dr. Wentworth. At last he said, "Within two or three days I should be able to give you a satisfactory answer. At present I dwell in ignorance. I had but an hour or two this afternoon to examine Mr. Povy, and to begin my enquiries. By tomorrow evening, or the evening after, I should be much better informed."

"But for *now*—how many do you think will die?" our minister insisted.

Uncle John consulted his wine again. Then he looked up and replied, "There will be several, I fear, and probably more. First in the village, and then wherever your panic-stricken parishioners might choose to flee. For after they have learned that the Plague has come to Branford, they will believe that flight is their best, and perhaps their only, hope of survival."

"That would be a dreadful thing if it were to happen," Thomas Wentworth said.

"Do you mean," said my mother, "that it would be dreadful if so many of the villagers were to die?"

"No, Mrs. Bullen, I do not mean that," he told her. "It would be a dreadful thing—a moral calamity, I think—if they were to flee from Branford to save themselves. By so doing, they would carry the Plague to other places where there is no Plague now."

"But undoubtedly they will do just that," my father said.

"It's what I should do myself," my sister exclaimed, "if I were one of the village people!"

"And it *is* what many people did in London," I said. "The gentry, of course, but others also. I saw them leaving—their goods, and household pets, and everything else, piled on top of their carts and wagons!"

"Perhaps the people of Branford will do as others have done," Thomas Wentworth said. "But perhaps they will not!"

Then he rose from the table and left us without another word. And not one of us had an inkling of what thoughts might have been in his mind, or why his expression should have been so fixed and strange, as he set off for the path that would lead to his village home.

Dangerous Silks

Uncle John went into Branford early the next morning and did not return until the late afternoon. When he did, he beckoned me to follow him to the back of the house, and there on the lawn he deposited the small package he had been carrying.

"Niece Eleanor," he said, "I now must bathe and change my clothing, as a precaution, for I have been with the Plague today. I shall return shortly, however, and then the three of us—you, your father, and I—shall examine the contents of that package. In the meantime I place *you* in charge of it. Let no one disturb it, and above all—do not touch it yourself, as you value your life!"

I was, of course, immediately consumed with a vast curiosity, but still I did manage to obey his admonition and left the package untouched. After a time he returned with my father, who eyed the package and said, with a quizzical lift of his eyebrow, "Well, John, is *this* to be the object of our momentous inquiry?"

"It is," Uncle John replied. He spread a blanket on the lawn and placed the package in the middle of it. Then he stooped and very gingerly unwrapped the package, revealing inside several tightly folded pieces of red silk cloth, all most lovely and elegant.

"Oh!" I cried. "You've been looking about Mr. Povy's shop."

"Yes," said Uncle John. "You have sharp eyes, young lady. These pieces of silk are, indeed, from Mr. Povy's workshop—and we now must examine them closely."

He knelt on the grass and, with great caution, unfolded the first piece of silk. "This is the one I've already looked at," he said to my father. "And when I did, Richard—see what I found."

My father knelt beside him. After several moments he said very softly, "Well, isn't that interesting!"

They seemed to have forgotten *me*, so I said, "Please, may I look too?"

Uncle John gave his assent, and I bent over and studied the lovely red silk. All at once I saw it—so small, so familiar, so insignificant!

"Why, *that* can't be what you found!" I said. "It's only a little dead flea!"

"That is exactly what I found," my uncle replied. "Now let us see if the other silk pieces also contain some dead fleas, for though I have not yet inspected them, I do imagine that they might."

One by one he unfolded the silks, and therein we

discovered six more fleas, all just as dead as the first. At that point my father began to shake his head, and he smiled grimly.

"You have guessed the direction of my thoughts?" asked Uncle John.

"I believe I may have," my father answered. "You told us that Mr. Povy had not been to London and, therefore, had not caught the Plague while visiting there. Now it seems that London—and the Plague—might have visited Mr. Povy here in Branford."

"Precisely," my uncle said. Then he took from his pocket a small empty vial and, again using great caution, placed the seven dead fleas inside it, without once touching any of them.

"Do you mean," I said, feeling considerably puzzled, "that Mr. Povy ordered the silk pieces from a merchant in London? And that after they arrived here, the fleas that were inside jumped out and bit him and gave him the Plague?"

"No, I think that only the first part of your account is true," my uncle told me. "That Mr. Povy ordered the silk from London is quite certain. And that there were no less than seven fleas inside the silk is equally certain too. However, it is inconceivable that those fleas were still alive, and bit him, when he opened his purchase here in Branford."

"But," my father said, "how can you be so sure that the fleas already were dead by then?"

"It's quite simple," my uncle explained. "A flea cannot live without air for very long—it will suffocate. And it cannot live more than a few days without food—without drinking the blood of a man or an animal—and those fleas had obtained no nourishment for almost a month. Consider it—they did not eat in London while they were packed inside the silk pieces, and they did not eat on the long, slow road to Branford. Nor did they eat in Mr. Povy's shop, where—he told me—he left the package unopened for at least two weeks after its arrival. In all, no less than the better part of a month without food! No—those fleas had long since starved to death when Mr. Povy finally opened the package and examined his beautiful red silk."

"But, Uncle John, if the fleas were already dead, how *did* he catch the Plague?" I asked. "Surely one cannot catch it from a *dead* flea!"

Uncle John held up the vial. "We must examine our specimens," he said, "and see what—if anything—they may have to tell us."

Together we filed into my father's laboratory. While I watched with marveling curiosity, my uncle brought out a cutting instrument and most skillfully dissected one of the dead fleas. Finally he placed a tiny portion of its entrails under my father's microscope.

Uncle John then peered into the eyepiece for what seemed an eternity. At last he whispered, "My friend, look at this—and tell me what you think."

Again there was silence as my father took his turn at the microscope. Finally he said, "Good Lord, John! But who could imagine that such a thing is possible?"

"Please," I said, "may I look too?"

My father stepped aside, I took my place at the microscope, and almost immediately I saw some of them!
Slowly, but beyond dispute, they were moving, twisting,
wriggling! They were still alive, inside the dead flea—the
tiny animals that were the bearers of fevers and swellings,
of delirium and death—the all-but-invisible carriers of
the Plague!

"Then did Mr. Povy somehow catch the Plague," I
said, "by touching the dead fleas?"

"I have little doubt of it," my uncle replied. "I examined Mr. Povy's hands yesterday and discovered a deep
cut in one of his thumbs. I asked him, Had he opened the
package and looked into it? He had! Did he recall seeing
any dead fleas inside? He did! In fact, he'd picked up
several and cast them away—he distinctly remembered
having disposed of several of the dead insects!"

Uncle John sighed and shook his head. "I cannot, of
course, prove it absolutely, but I'm quite certain that
while handling the infected fleas, and all unaware of the
awful danger he was in, Mr. Povy unwittingly crushed
one of them between his thumb and finger—as I once,
young lady, cautioned *you* against doing. Some of the tiny
animals we have just seen under the microscope entered
Mr. Povy's blood through the cut in his thumb, and infected him with the Plague."

"And now," I said, "because of that simple mischance,
the poor man will almost surely die."

My uncle shook his head once more. "No, your tense is
wrong, Niece Eleanor. Mr. Povy died an hour ago."

And then I heard the sound that we were to hear often that summer and autumn, the doleful sound of the village bell tolling for the dead.

The Path of Light

Within hours of Mr. Povy's death, anxiety and bewilderment began to grip the inhabitants of Branford village. The Plague had come and struck down their hardworking neighbor—but did that necessarily mean others would sicken and die? Sixty or seventy families, perhaps three hundred people in all, were at risk—but who could say how great that risk really was?

The next day Uncle John went down to the village and, accompanied by Mr. Ford, the apothecary, walked about and visited the sick. Three people were ill with the Plague, he told us that evening, and it was his belief that they would probably die very soon. Three others exhibited what might be early symptoms of the disease. Fear now could be seen in the faces of many villagers, and panic seemed not far away.

At Branford Hall there was growing fear and anxiety too. My mother, chiefly concerned with the safety of her family, decreed that my sister and I were not to enter the village under any circumstances. I was, however, permitted to cross the stone bridge above the village stream and, on the far side, to sit in the comforting shade of an oak tree with Kate. There we exchanged all manner of tales and rumors about the terrible drama that was unfolding before our eyes.

My mother's fears, though, were not limited to her two daughters. Had she been able, she would have compelled Uncle John to give up his visits to Branford village as well. But he, of course, coolly shrugged off her concern for his safety. He reminded her that he was, after all, an experienced physician, the situation in the village was approaching a crisis, and his presence there was surely required. He would, nevertheless, take every precaution to protect himself from the contagion, and promised to avoid all unncessary risks.

But when my father said one morning, in the most careless, offhand way, that he intended to accompany Uncle John on his next visit to the sick and dying, my mother's feelings overflowed. She grew so red in the face that I feared she was having an attack of the apoplexy.

"How can you even think of doing so?" she cried. "How can you think of placing yourself in danger without any rhyme or reason? Have I not endured enough already? Have I not lost Samuel and Henry? And now, through mere idle foolishness, am I to lose my husband as well? Am I to be left a widow simply because your ever-lasting curiosity is goading and bestirring you once more?"

After this outburst my father was immediately over-come with contrition, and he gave my mother his solemn oath that he would abandon all such selfish notions. He would remain at home, as she requested, safe from all danger.

Then on Sunday morning, without the slightest hint of what lay ahead, Thomas Wentworth arose in the pulpit of his village church and delivered the most extra-ordinary sermon of his life. Kate was seated in one of the crowded pews, and from her I afterwards learned what had transpired.

Our minister—her uncle—seemed transformed. Never before had he looked so tall, so magisterial, so command-ing. Everyone observed that he was unusually pale, and some thought it was with the holy, sacred paleness of the saints and martyrs. And his voice, miraculously, was not set at its usual high pitch but was low and sonorous, and seemed to vibrate with a hypnotic resonance that it never had previously possessed.

"The Plague is now among us," he began, and then he spoke with feeling of Samuel Povy's virtues, his death, and the sickness of others in the village.

"That some of us will die of the Plague is certain," he said, "and that some of us will survive is certain too. One question only remains for us to determine: What will we, the people of Branford, decide to do in the face of this sudden affliction?

The Path of Light

"There are but two paths open to us. The first is the Dark Path. The path of fear and panic, of selfishness and self-concern. If we follow *that* path, we will flee our homes and become scattered, like flocks of carrion crows, across the countryside. We will carry the Plague to other villages and towns, bringing sickness and death to legions of unsuspecting families. To men, women, and innocent babes who have never harmed us and have never wished us the slightest ill.

"The second path open to us is the Path of Light. The path of courage and selflessness, of spiritual grace and high moral splendor. If we follow *this* path, we will remain in our homes; we will seal ourselves up, so that nobody leaves or enters our village until the Plague is over. We will pray to the Lord for guidance and strength and, by our conduct, will set an example for the world that will be long remembered."

Thomas Wentworth paused then, and the sunlight, streaming in through the chancel window, seemed to grow even brighter around his head.

"I shall remain here with you," he said at last. "I shall follow the Path of Light, the good path, the path of the Lord. And I pray that all of you, each and every one, will choose to remain with me here in Branford, and by remaining will secure for your immortal souls Grace and Glory for all eternity!"

The Reverend Thomas Wentworth paused again, then said, "Amen," very quietly, and in the little church there was a silence so profound that afterwards people said they had never heard any silence quite like it.

Faith over Reason

Later that day Thomas Wentworth slowly climbed the hill from the village and joined our family as we sat together on the grassy lawn behind the house. My mother had already heard about our minister's Sunday-morning sermon, and her religious sentiments had been deeply touched. She greeted her future son-in-law with what seemed to me a new respect that amounted almost to deference.

"It is a valiant and noble venture that you have proposed," she said. "I cannot remember anything to equal it. You have brought great credit upon yourself today!"

My father nodded and said, "No one can doubt the nobility of your proposal, Thomas, nor question your idealism." Then in a slightly ironic tone he continued, "*But*, as the father of your betrothed, I am obliged to add that I do hope the people of Branford prove to be less noble and selfless than you. In that case some of them will act to save themselves, and will flee the village, and that in turn will permit you—in all good conscience—to look to your own safety as well."

And Uncle John said, "As a man of science, Dr. Wentworth, I can speak very little about faith and idealism, or the nobility of self-sacrifice. But this much I *can* say—that the village people I have talked with and examined appeared to be ordinary men and women, of the sort one encounters any and every day of one's life. Nothing about them struck me as particularly noble, selfless, or high-minded. And so I believe that before long, you will discover that your sermon has fallen on deaf ears. Soon the first flock of carrion crows will fly in panic out of Branford, to infect our neighboring towns and villages and ultimately, perhaps, to spread the Plague to every last corner of the kingdom."

Our minister had looked weary enough when he'd arrived, the strain of the morning all too evident in his heavy tread and the exaggerated stoop of his shoulders. Now, under the impact of my uncle's words, much of his remaining strength and self-assurance seemed to drain away.

Seeing this, my sister went to him and took his hand. "I disagree with your detractors," she said. "I believe, as you do, that the villagers will prove strong and resolute. What did they say, Tom, after morning service? Did not some of them express admiration for your eloquence and vision?"

Her words, and the touch of her hand, appeared to restore him. Or else it was her adoring glance, so filled with the love and pride that she made no effort to conceal.

"My parishioners," he told her, "said very little after the service. I think most were too surprised to say anything. Later, though, William Ford and John Watson did come to the rectory. They said that they and the other vestrymen had agreed to meet later in the morning, to consider what steps—if any—should be taken."

Our minister paused and then looked across at Uncle John. "I may be mistaken," he said, "but I thought there was something in their manner that suggested my words might not have fallen on deaf ears after all."

Thomas Wentworth shook his head and then went on. "But no matter what the people of Branford should decide, all of us in the village are faced with a terrible affliction, unlike anything we have ever encountered before. And so, Dr. Townley, I have come here this afternoon to seek your advice. You have seen the Plague in London. What can you tell us that will be of help in dealing with whatever trials we shall have to endure?"

Uncle John thought for a time and then said, "I can give you six simple rules that will increase your parishioners' chance of survival. The First Rule: Use all medicine sparingly, for there is not one that will prevent or cure the Plague.

"Rule Two: Pay no heed to quack remedies, magical nostrums, or superstitious hocus-pocus. Smearing yourself with some evil-smelling unguent will not ward off the disease, nor will the burning of incense keep you safe.

"Rule Three: Kill all household animals without exception. Dogs, cats, pigeons, the entire lot. And move all livestock into the fields. In London, so I've been told, no less than 50,000 dogs alone were killed this past spring and early summer, and I believe that it helped reduce the death toll immeasurably."

Here I cringed at the thought that my own dear Royal would have had to die if we lived in the village. I believe I must have prayed that entire night, thanking God that I was not a villager, and also asking Him to comfort those who would lose a dear pet.

Uncle John continued. "Rule Four: Both the bedding and the apparel of the dead should be destroyed. You must burn or bury them, and under *no* circumstances should either be washed or cleaned and then used again.

"Rule the Fifth: Anyone attending the sick or the dead must wash his hands thoroughly, immediately after such work is done. I fear, though, that because of habit, few of your parishioners will do so willingly, if, indeed, they will do so at all."

Then Uncle John smiled his wintry smile and said, "Last but not least, Rule Six: Close up your church, Dr. Wentworth, and preach no more sermons there until the Plague has departed. A crowded church is one of the finest places for infected fleas to crawl or jump from the clothing of one host to another. Let there be no tightly packed crowds inside your church, and those carriers of disease and death will be able to do much less harm."

Before Uncle John could add anything further, we saw two figures approaching over the rise of the hill. One was

William Ford, and the other was John Watson. Mr. Ford looked cool enough following his climb, but Mr. Watson was sweating mightily.

Chairs were brought out for our visitors, and once they were seated, they began to glance questioningly at one another, each evidently reluctant to be the spokesman now. At last Mr. Watson wiped off his streaming forehead and looked at our minister.

"We have discussed your proposal at our vestry meeting," he said in a low and solemn voice. "And it is our decision that we must, in our faith, seal ourselves up inside Branford village, no matter what the cost, until such time as the Plague is gone. It is our belief that to pass the Plague on to others would be to commit an unpardonable evil, and by the commission of it to risk the salvation of our immortal souls."

Very softly, Thomas Wentworth said, "You speak for the vestry council—but what of the others? Will most people in the village accept your decision?"

"At first," John Watson replied, "a few were hesitant or reluctant. But now, after further discussion, everyone in the village has agreed to remain. The people of Branford have made their choice, Dr. Wentworth, and it is to follow the Path of Light."

My father and Uncle John sat unmoving, silent and astonished. My mother and Mary sat silent too, their faces lit with awe and exaltation. Our minister bowed his head, and I saw his lips move as though in prayer.

Then he turned to our visitors. "Thank you, my friends," he said. "If you will join me in the rectory early this evening—say at five o'clock—we can begin to draw up plans for isolating ourselves inside Branford village, and for maintaining ourselves there as best we can until the Plague has left."

And then, in a voice that was scarcely a whisper, he said, "Lord have mercy upon us"—the very words I had seen, that terrible evening in St. Giles, inscribed on the doors of those who were dying of the Plague.

23

Rebellion!

Seldom had I found the world more uncertain and confusing than I did on that memorable Sunday afternoon. Like my father and Uncle John, I had supposed that our local villagers would spurn the idealistic vision of their minister and flee in panic from their homes, as once I had seen the terrified inhabitants of London fleeing theirs.

But the people of Branford had determined to act otherwise. They had agreed to risk their lives for the sake of their principles. And by so doing, they had called into question much of what I thought I knew about the way ordinary people behave in the face of danger.

What I found even more perplexing, though, was my own sister's state of mind. Clearly she was ecstatic that her beloved's plan had been accepted by the villagers, while apparently ignoring the fact that its acceptance might very well lead to his death. In her place I would have preferred my future husband to be a little less high-minded and selfless, and a little more careful of his own good health, lest one day I find myself unwed, bereft, and heartbroken.

And so when we had a moment together inside the house, I said, "Mary, I do believe I understand how you feel about Thomas's noble proposal. Yet I do not understand how you can disregard the danger in which he is placing himself. You appear entirely calm and serene this afternoon. But you must realize that the danger is great—how can you behave as though it does not even trouble you?"

Her expression was solemn as she said to me, "Oh Nell, the danger, of course, is great. But he will survive, I know, and so in the end everything will be well."

Her reply only added to my bewilderment. Choosing my words with care, I said, "Survive? But how can anyone say with certainty who will survive and who will not?"

My sister's lovely dark eyes began to gleam with a passionate intensity. "I shall pray for him!" she said, taking my hand. "I shall pray to the Lord, and I know that in His infinite goodness He will spare His servant!"

I said nothing after that, for I realized no words of mine could change her opinion, or alter her state of mind. And I knew as well that her faith was not only far greater than mine but was of a different order altogether, so that, in truth, I scarcely could comprehend it.

As I sat outside on the lawn again, my thoughts soon turned from my sister to Thomas Wentworth, her betrothed. There he was, but a few feet away, talking with my father. The villagers, he said, would need supplies from time to time, and arrangements should be made in advance for obtaining them. All of this he stated in an easy, conversational tone, as though he were merely discussing the purchase of some food for the parish house, and not for a band of desperate country people who soon enough would be suffering from a fatal disease.

And then it struck me: The curious fact that except for Uncle John, it was I who knew more about the frightfulness that lay ahead than did anyone else in Branford. For I, and I alone, had been to St. Giles and seen the horrors of the Plague with my own eyes.

I looked at our minister again and wondered whether he really understood what he had set in motion, and I wondered, too, who in the village was fated to die? Would it be John Watson and William Ford, the two vestrymen who had just appeared at Branford Hall? Would it be one or another of the three boys I studied with at our village school? Or would Thomas Wentworth's niece, my own beloved friend Kate, be sacrificed to her uncle's noble ideals and fine principles?

It was the thought of Kate's death that transformed me then, and I found myself filled with so hot and deep a fury that it astonished me. I clenched my fists and bit my lower lip, lest I give a sudden and most unwise vent to this fury at our minister, whose high-mindedness might so easily cost my friend her life.

I knew that I must calm myself, and this I did manage to do, breathing deeply and slowly several times and looking away at the ground with a blank stare. At last I felt in command of myself again, and when there was a pause in the conversation around me, I spoke to Thomas Wentworth. "Something puzzles me, and I wonder if I might ask you about it. I am very young, and ignorant of many things, but perhaps you will forgive my ignorance because of my youth."

"What puzzles you, Nell?" he said. "If I can help clear your mind in any way, or resolve any doubts you may have, either spiritual or worldly, I shall gladly do so."

"Well, it is true, is it not," I said, "that most people in the village would have nowhere to go, even if they wished to flee?"

"Yes," he replied, "that is perfectly true."

"But what if someone in the village *did* have a place to go? What if there were loving friends who would gladly take that person in and save that person from the Plague?"

We looked into each other's eyes, and I do not know what he beheld in mine, for I was attempting to appear innocent, worshipful, and artless.

"Do you have some particular person in mind?" he asked me.

I took a last deep breath for its calming affect, and I said, "Yes, I do. My friend Kate, your niece. She would be welcome here at Branford Hall, I know. She would be safe from the Plague, and I cannot think of any reason why she should not come to us this very day!"

Our minister sighed heavily and looked down at me with what I believe was the saddest smile I ever did see.

"Unhappily," he said, "there is a very good reason why

Kate should not come to you here. What would the village people say if she did? They would say to me, 'You have asked us to place our own lives at risk, yet you have permitted your niece to avoid the danger!' And they would repudiate their pledge, and before long many would flee their homes, to sleep in the open fields or in the houses of strangers. They would carry the Plague with them—the Lord only knows how far and wide—and innumerable thousands might very well suffer and die because of their flight."

He sighed again, and said, "I wish with all my heart that she could come to stay with you here, but dear Nell, that must not be!"

He turned away from me, and I was surprised once more at the depths of my anger. I did *not* agree. I would *not* give in! Somehow, in some way, I would save my friend Kate—and I immediately began to consider how I might do so!

Mय Scheme to Save Kate

For the rest of that afternoon I schemed in secret, devising what I believed was a marvelous plan to rescue my friend. At the same time, I pretended to have nothing more on my mind than what my elders sometimes called "the usual idle thoughts of the young."

Finally the hour approached for my meeting with Kate. I ambled slowly across the lawn and along the lane that led to the village until I was out of sight of the house. Then I sped downhill at a great pace and ran the last few yards over the bridge, arriving at our rendezvous with heart pounding and much out of breath.

Kate was there awaiting me. Her eyes were tired, her expression somber. Preparations already had begun in the village, she told me—food was being gathered and stored, and signs would soon be posted in a ring around Branford, warning strangers not to enter because of the

Plague. Most grim of all, spades and shovels were being collected by the vestry council. And so no matter how many graves might have to be dug, there surely would be a sufficient number for the task.

"I cannot stay here very long," she said. "There is much work to be done in the parish house, and I must return there and help my mother."

Then she smiled—most bravely, I thought—and said, "This is good-bye for now, Nell. After today I'll not be permitted to leave the village to meet anyone, and so will be unable to come here and talk with you this way. Nor will I be able to write anything to you, for fear of giving you the Plague. It is said that we in the village soon will have Death itself upon our fingers and hands, and any letter from me would not be safe for you to handle.

"But if you will come here at the same time each day," she went on, "I'll watch for you, and try to signal from inside the village. And if ever you should care to leave a letter or a written message for me, I shall come and fetch it after you've gone."

She smiled again, said, "Good-bye, Nell," and stood up to go.

"No, Kate," I said. "Do but wait a moment—I have things of great importance to tell you!" I quickly described my talk with her uncle, and how it had inflamed me and set my mind to working. I said that I had no intention of sitting idly by, with her in grave danger, and I'd devised a plan to transport her from the village to a place of safety, and so to rescue her from the Plague.

"Rescue me from the Plague?" she said, her eyes growing wide. "But I'm not in any need of being rescued."

"Of course you are!" I cried. "I have been to London, and have seen what the Plague really is. Do not argue with me now. You must not remain in Branford village an hour longer than necessary!"

"You would have me flee? But where should I run away to?"

"To Branford Hall," I said. "And this very night. Listen to my plan: After everyone in the village is asleep, you must slip out of the parish house and meet me here, in this same spot—say at midnight. And we will go back to the Hall together, and there I will hide you in the barn that stands near the pond. It is very little used, and so will be a perfect place for your concealment."

"You would have me sleep in your barn?"

"Why, of course," I said. "There is hay stored there, and one can burrow down into it for warmth, and sleep quite well, I'm sure. And tonight, before I meet you, I will put some blankets there as well, and so you will be very comfortable."

"And for how long shall I live in the barn?"

"Until the Plague is over."

"And my food and drink?"

"I'll bring them to you every day," I said. "I am always out of doors, seeing that Royal has his proper exercise, so no one will think anything of my visiting the barn now and then. And that's when I'll bring you the food I take from the kitchen, which I can do most easily. And also I shall bring you water in a bottle or flask, hiding it beneath some of my garments, as best I can arrange."

She stared at me, saying not a word, and so I plunged ahead. "And if it should prove too cold for you in the barn," I said, "because autumn comes, and the Plague is still in the village, why then, we can exchange places every night or two. You can sleep in my bed in the Hall, and I will stay in the barn. In that way we will both keep strong and healthy, and not grow sick with the chilblains or other diseases of the cold."

"You have devised a perfect plan for saving me, have you not?" she said.

"I have," said I.

Then my friend laughed a very kindly laugh, with not a trace of malice in it, and she said, "Poor dear Nell. So clever and wise in some things, and so foolish in others."

"Are you saying that my plan is foolish?" I asked her.

"It's a very kind and generous plan," she said. "But it really is foolish also. It could never succeed—we'd be caught very quickly. Either somebody would see one of us lurking around the barn, or else your mother would notice how the food was disappearing from her kitchen. And besides, Uncle Thomas is right—I *must* stay in the village. For if I do not, after my flight is discovered, some of the people there surely will run away, and spread the Plague across the countryside. Yet it is strange, is it not, that the lives of so many people should depend on what a simple country girl decides to do, on such a lovely summer evening as this one?"

"Then you won't let me help you?" I said.

"Not in the way you mean," she replied. "The only way you can help me is if you will leave a message for me from time to time. And also leave a letter from your sister to Uncle Thomas, for he will be most anxious to hear from her, I'm sure."

I watched her leave, cross to the parish house, pause for a moment, and disappear inside. Then I began to walk around the perimeter of the village. I saw that the first stakes already had been driven into the ground, and that on several there was a picture painted of a skull with crossed bones, a warning signal to strangers not to enter. It was the beginning of the Circle of Death that the villagers were drawing around themselves.

I shuddered, for the evening seemed to have grown colder, and then I turned away from the village and started to climb back up the hill to Branford Hall.

The Bell Tolls in Branford

That night I dreamed once more that I was back in St. Giles. But instead of the kindly, white-haired Reverend Robert Frith standing on the steps of the parish church, it was the madwoman standing there and crying out, "Where is my daughter? Where is my sweet Kate? I am saving her a place in The Death Cart!" Many nights thereafter I dreamed the same dream, or some bizarre variation of it. And always I was in St. Giles, and always the madwoman was there, calling out for my friend.

Night and day, thoughts of the Plague haunted all of us living at Branford Hall. How could it have been otherwise? We knew that below us, in the valley, only a mile or so away, people were sickening and dying. Each day we remembered their suffering, and prayed for their safety, while going about our daily tasks.

My mother still had the manor house to run, and Mary and I helped her whenever she required us to. Each morning, as always, I practiced for an hour on her harpsichord, and for that hour at least, because my thoughts were solely of the music, my spirits lifted and I enjoyed a brief spell of contentment.

Every day, morning and afternoon, I took Royal out for his exercise. Sometimes I walked down the lane that led directly to the village, and there left some words for Kate as well as Mary's daily letter for her betrothed. Sometimes I took the opposite way, high up along the base of Eagles' Roost, and so went around to the far side of Branford. This I did each Sunday, and watched the villagers far below, gathered together in a little hollow, a natural amphitheater, where Thomas Wentworth held services for his flock. The village church remained empty and unused because of the contagion.

My father was especially busy now, his chief purpose being to make sure that every village family possessed enough food and other necessities during this time of awful trial. He and my mother gave generously and were glad they could do so—one week donating flour or tools, another week feed for the villagers' livestock.

The villagers, though, were extremely proud, and they often paid for what they required, leaving their silver and copper coins at a designated place in the stream. There, for a day or two, the coins would lie uncollected, while the waters of the stream supposedly washed away whatever contagious matter might have been left on them by the villagers' infected hands. Afterwards, someone would retrieve them from the water, though never very willingly, for everyone feared that the coins might yet be contaminated.

~ ~ ~

Almost every day that summer, the church bell tolled in the village, and each time we heard it, those of us at Branford Hall could not help but wonder whether or not one of our particular friends had died. And most often we thought of the family in the parish house. For my sister the sound of the suddenly tolling bell must have been a fearful sound indeed.

By the middle of August, the Povy family was no more. Mrs. Povy, who so often had given Kate and me sweet cakes in her friendly kitchen; Jasper, a healthy, vigorous youth; and poor frail little Arthur, huddling by the fireplace to keep warm—all three were gone now.

Near the end of August, Captain Dunstan buried his son, "Pinching Will." A few days later the captain was seen lying in a doorway, his hat pulled down over his eyes, apparently sleeping off a heavy draft of alcoholic spirits. But that was not so—he'd been overcome by the symptoms of the Plague while walking through the village, sat down to recover himself, and within an hour or two had expired.

It seemed that chance alone determined who would live or die. At the inn, John Watson and his wife survived untouched, though they had less business to occupy them now. For the London coach no longer stopped at Branford village. Instead, it drove down the High Street without pause, past the warning fence of skulls and bones, and then sped on to the inn at Upper Whitcombe, several miles away.

William Ford, the village apothecary, remained in good health, but his wife was not so fortunate. She always had seemed healthy enough—I well remembered how ruddy she had looked the last time I'd seen her, a basket of leeks swaying under her arm, as she strode along the street. Nevertheless, the Plague soon caught her, and she was dead in less than three days' time.

Andrew Goodfellow, our blacksmith, so strong and hearty, should have been safe against the infection, but the bell tolled for him during the first week in September. And wiry young Oliver Robinson, the village cobbler—it seemed only yesterday, on a fair summer's afternoon, that I had watched him in front of the inn, dancing about and cursing because a wasp had just stung him on the wrist. Now he'd been stung by a far deadlier enemy, and in late September the bell also tolled for him.

~ ~ ~

Yet even in the midst of all these sad and terrible things, one thought continued to cheer me—Kate remained well. And for a few minutes each afternoon we were able to wave and call a few words to one another, she from behind the Circle of Death inside the village, and I from across the way, outside it. And I knew that after I had departed, she would come over and take the letters I left for her, as well as the sweet cakes or some other treat from our kitchen or larder.

Then one afternoon, she did not appear at the usual

hour. No matter, I told myself, today she must have some extra work that occupies her. But when, the next afternoon, she did not appear again, and I discovered that the previous day's letters remained uncollected, I began to be filled with the worst sort of dread.

That night, before sleep, I knelt by the side of my bed and prayed to the Lord that my friend be spared, and that it was not sickness which twice now had kept her away from our rendezvous.

Then I did something I had not done for ages: I went to the little chest where I kept my treasures and took out the enamel portrait of my uncle Edgar, whose eyes looked so much like those of my brother Henry. As I had done when I was much younger, I carried it back to bed, and after putting out my candle, I held it under my pillow. And I prayed again for Kate, and for every other child in Branford village, and for poor sick children everywhere who were in danger and in need of prayers. But in my heart I believed that my friend was sick with the Plague, and that never again would I see her alive.

Red Cross on the Parish House Door

Late that night, a great blustery autumn storm arrived. For the next several days, it rained so hard that I was forced to keep indoors at Branford Hall, and could not go down to the village road to seek my friend. As each stormy day passed, my spirits grew heavier, and I became more certain that Kate was dead. And when the weather finally cleared, and I was able to rush down the muddy, leaf-strewn lane to the village, what I saw there seemed to confirm my fears.

She had not come from the parish house to retrieve the two small baskets I had left for her before the storm. The peaches from our orchard were spoiled and beginning to grow moldy. A small Dutch cheese, of the kind that I knew she loved, had been discovered by some wild animal, and lay upon the ground, much gnawed and devoured. My sister's two letters to Thomas Wentworth, and my own two notes of gossip and cheer, all lay caked and sodden in the bottoms of the baskets.

She has not come to fetch them, I thought, because she is dead.

As I paced slowly around, outside the warning fence of skulls and bones, my eyes were caught by a flash of color on the door of the parish house. I suddenly realized that a red cross was painted there.

I stood frozen in my tracks, when the door of the parish house edged open. A figure stepped out. To my utter disbelief, I saw it was Kate!

She began to walk toward me, and I was shocked by how much she had changed, how pale and sickly she looked.

"Kate!" I cried. "What has happened? There is a red cross on the door."

She put her hand to her mouth as though to keep herself from speaking. At last she said, "It was placed there for my mother. She died three days ago."

"Oh Kate, how terrible!" I said.

My friend did not reply for a long time. Finally, she said, "My mother suffered very little, Nell, thank the good Lord. And it does seem that neither Uncle Thomas not I have been affected, and in that there is something to be grateful for."

I was left speechless—awed by her courage, which I knew so much exceeded my own.

I promised to return the next day, we said good-bye, and I trudged back home, my mind much tormented and distressed by what I had learned. At Branford Hall I found my parents and Uncle John, and my sister, all gathering together for supper, and I told them about Kate's mother, Mrs. Carter.

They were thunderstruck and appalled, and my sister was especially affected. "Poor Tom," she said. "It must hurt him grievously. I wonder if he will ever be able to forgive himself."

"What about Kate?" I said. "She is an orphan now, and has no one to support or protect her, save only her uncle! What will become of her?"

"Do not fret about that, Nell," my mother said quickly. "Kate will be well looked after and protected. She is, in truth, all but a member of our family now." And then my mother gave me further words of comfort, for she remembered that it still was my childish wont to burst into tears when too overwrought, and she wished to avoid having this happen on so dark and mournful an occasion.

~ ~ ~

Kate's mother was very nearly the last person to die of the Plague in Branford village. Uncle John, shortly before he returned to London, had foreseen that such might be the case. In the capital, he told us, cooler weather had prevailed for several weeks, and as a consequence, the Plague had almost entirely disappeared there.

"I believe it will be much the same in Branford," he said. "This week's storm has brought an end to the summer heat, and I have no doubt that with cooler weather, you soon will see an end to the Plague here."

And so it happened—the village bell tolled less and less frequently, until finally, by mid-October, it ceased tolling altogether.

~ ~ ~

One autumn afternoon my mother took me aside and talked with me about Kate's future—and my own.

"I have spoken with Thomas Wentworth," she said, "and he agrees with me, Nell, that in a week or two, the Plague now behind us, your friend Kate should come and live here at Branford Hall. It will be far better than having her remain in the village, where so many memories must be very painful for her.

"As for *your* future, Nell," my mother continued, "I have been giving it much consideration. And I have been in correspondence with your uncle George Townley, in London."

"The schoolmaster?" I said.

My mother nodded. "I think it might be best for you to spend the coming winter in London, attending George's school for girls. And perhaps—if your father and I should so decide—Kate might also attend the school and be your companion there."

"A school in London?" I said. "Do you really think Kate and I might go?"

"We shall see, we shall see," my mother said. But I knew—for I had learned to judge such things quite nicely—that her mind most likely was made up already, and that Kate and I would go to London one day, to attend my uncle George's Academy for Young Ladies.

27

Journey's End

One afternoon the following week, Kate and I left the parish house and set out to gather some late wildflowers to place on her mother's grave.

As we walked along, I could see in the village the first signs of recovery—the wooden stakes, with their skulls and bones, had been taken down and removed; the Circle of Death around the village was gone. And the inn was becoming a more congenial and bustling place again. The London coach now stopped there daily and gave strangers a glimpse of Branford—the village that had kept the Plague from spreading by isolating itself from the rest of the world.

Still, there were marks enough of the Plague's cruel devastation—any number of red crosses remained on the doors of the houses. And several of those houses showed no signs of life within—no smoke from a chimney, no mother or child in a doorway enjoying the sun's warmth, no man with his tools setting out on his afternoon's labors.

Kate and I gathered what flowers we could find and then walked to the village graveyard. A large rectangle of earth was there, recently turned, and Kate said to me, "That is the common grave."

"I didn't know there had been one," I replied.

"Uncle Thomas authorized it, for he had no choice. There were too few able-bodied men left, when the Plague was at its height. Exactly as you told me it was in London."

"But not your mother?" I said.

She shook her head and led me to the far side of the graveyard, to a temporary wooden cross with her mother's name written on it. We placed the flowers there, and Kate said, "I believe she died because she visited the sick and cared for them. She would not let me go with her, though. She said it was too dangerous, and made me stay home."

I looked around the graveyard and said, "How many died in the village, do you think?"

"More than a hundred, Uncle Thomas says."

"And how do people feel now?"

"Full of woe and sadness," Kate told me. "But also proud, for they know they have done an extraordinary thing."

"And your uncle?"

Kate looked down at the grave and sighed. "He comes here every day," she said, "and mourns for his sister. He knows that she might still be alive if he had acted differently. I always can tell when he's visited here, because his eyes are red from weeping when he returns."

We left the graveyard and once more circled the village, enjoying the cool, sunlit afternoon. And as we did, we began to talk about what things might lie ahead.

"It will be good to have you living in Branford Hall," I told her. "Even though it may not be for long."

"And then on to London," Kate said. "It will seem very strange living there, Nell. But still, I'd like to do that now."

"You told me once that you loved it here in Branford so much," I said, "that you didn't want to go anywhere else—that has changed, hasn't it?"

"It has," she said. "My feelings about Branford have changed a great deal in the last few weeks."

"Yes, I can see that," I said. "Your uncle's eyes aren't the only ones that are red from weeping."

A week or so later Kate settled in with us at Branford Hall and very quickly became one of the family. I soon asked her how she liked living in the manor house, and she said that indeed, she liked it very much.

"My room is most agreeable," she said.

Then she grinned mischievously, as I had not seen her do for many weeks, and said, "Yes, I like living in Branford Hall—and Nell, it's much, much better than living in your *barn*!"

So I knew her spirits were better at last, and I gave her a great hug, and we laughed together, as we had not laughed for the longest time.

~ ~ ~

And there it is—the story of the Great London Plague and the people of Branford, as best I could tell it.

Now most of the actors are gone, save only for a few relics like me. But we few do remember still the fear and the horror, the bravery and the courage, of those desperate times.

And we last survivors have many happier memories too. For myself there were the kindly people of Branford, who welcomed that wide-eyed young girl who came among them. And there was my family, of course, who loved me so generously—my studious father, my watchful mother, my ever warmhearted sister, and the brother I lost much too soon.

And there *was* one more—my dear, true friend Kate— braver than I, better than I—what splendid memories come back whenever I think of her cheerful voice, her sparkling eyes, and above all—her mischievous grin!

A Note for the Reader

The story of Eleanor Bullen, her family, and Branford village is set in England during the Restoration—the period beginning in 1660, when the Stuart kings returned to power. It was a period of foreign wars and domestic catastrophes—in 1665 London suffered its last epidemic of the Plague, and the next year a vast part of the old city burned to the ground in the Great Fire. While few if any people died in the fire, countless thousands died of the Plague, a disease for which there was no cure and of which most people were terrified; in some ways at least, it was the AIDS of its time.

Almost all the characters in *Nell of Branford Hall* are entirely fictional, but there are exceptions. Sir Christopher Wren, Robert Boyle, and Isaac Newton, guests at Branford Hall, were among the most famous men of their age; and Samuel Pepys and Sir John Evelyn were two leading citizens, and the keepers of famous diaries—they appear in the story much as they really were.

The fictional village of Branford is modeled on a real English village called Eyam. There, in 1665, things happened as I have described them, and the village people really did what they do in this story—improbable as that may seem to us today.

Acknowledgments

I would like to express my thanks to several friends who read *Nell of Branford Hall* and made helpful comments and suggestions: Peter and Virginia Binzen, Eleanor Clark, Claire and Nathan Kroll, Bradford and Mary Kelleher, Nora and Roger Shattuck, and Professor Eugene Waith, Yale University's eminent Shakespearean and Restoration scholar, who detected anachronisms and verbal infelicities with an unerring eye.

Also, my special thanks to my "young" reader, Jane Hamill, who met Nell Bullen months before anyone else, and whose enthusiasm was of more importance to the author than she will ever know.

Finally, my thanks to my editor and friend Diane Arico, who enabled Nell and her story to reach the public—she was, from first to last, absolutely indispensable.